I0736749

A Hole in the Air

First published in Great Britain in 2022 by:

Carnelian Heart Publishing Ltd
Suite A
82 James Carter Road
Mildenhall
Suffolk
IP28 7DE
UK

www.carnelianheartpublishing.co.uk

Paperback ISBN   978-1-914287-15-2
Ebook ISBN   978-1-914287-16-9

A CIP catalogue record for this book is available from the British Library.

Editors:
Samantha Rumbidzai Vazhure and Andrea Leeth

Cover:
Artwork: Nataleana
Design and layout: Lazarus Panashe Nyagwambo

Typeset by Carnelian Heart Publishing Ltd
Layout and formatting by DanTs Media

For those who get headaches trying to find answers, reasons, lessons and patterns; those who are dizzied by the speed of rotation of this little blue ball that becomes invisible at just 68 doublings of an A4 piece of paper; and those that have given up and adopted a lifestyle rooted in the words of the wisest of sages, "It is what it is."

This will do nothing to help you.

Contents

"…Our planet is a lonely speck in the great enveloping cosmic dark.

In our obscurity, in all this vastness, there is no hint that help will come from elsewhere to save us from ourselves…"

– Carl Sagan, Pale Blue Dot, 1994

The Woman in The Red Dress

The old AVM bus roars adamantly as it ambles along the dull grey tarmac, trailed by a short tail of thick, hazardous looking black smoke. Once upon a time, its chassis had been coated in bright yellow paint, but the years have weathered it to something closer to white. It is a vestige. It trembles subtly in that way that old buses do, determined to reach the end of yet another voyage despite its condition. At inclines, it slows almost to a crawl under the weight of the luggage piled haphazardly along the length of its roof: suitcases, duffel bags, baskets, sacks, *changani* bags with their fragile zippers stretched taut from the groceries stuffed inside them, and a single green wheelbarrow. At first glance the arrangement seems chaotic, precarious even, but it has been packed with all the expertise and ingenuity of a bus conductor. Nothing will fall off.

A rusty white sign stands stoically at the side of the road, jadedly welcoming travellers to the city of Rusape in big bold black letters. The driver presses his foot smoothly on the brakes to slow down for the city traffic. The bus continues to roar.

You are seated inside, by the window. Your head is resting against the pane which is decorated with greasy fingerprints, water streaks and dust. You watch unenthusiastically as the world zooms past the glass rectangle, an endless panorama that disappears behind you, into the past.

Sitting next to you is a thin, tired looking middle-aged woman with a fidgety toddler perched on her lap, facing your direction. The woman's head is thrown back and tilted slightly towards you and her eyes are closed. One of her eyes bulges alarmingly out of its socket and you do your best not to stare. Your grandmother told you that it is a sin to be repulsed by other people's deformities. You can hear her voice, "Laugh at someone else's deformity when you yourself have died." At the corner of the woman's mouth you can see a small head of froth. Since the woman got on the bus in Ruwa, the little boy's shoe has brushed against your thigh several times, leaving an atlas of brown smudges on your blue jeans. The little boy is eyeing you enviously, coveting your window seat. He kicks you again. The thing that has been sitting in your chest, the same thing that always accompanies you on these trips, starts to swell. You feel it push against your ribs and begin to crush your heart and your lungs. You clench your fists and close your eyes and breathe in, urgently.

One; a blue shoe.

Two; a torn, brown leather seat.

Three; a dirty window.

You exhale.

You turn to the woman and nudge her gently on her shoulder. She wakes with a start, and some drool streams down her chin. You wait for her to wipe it off before you speak. "*Mhamha,* your son has been stepping on my trousers. Look, they are already dirty." She stares at you for a little too long, the remnants of sleep still clinging to the flesh underneath her good eye. The other one seems discomfortingly cognizant, as if it sees everything, as if it never sleeps. She does not say anything to you, but she takes off the boy's shoes.

The memory invades you. It permeates your mind almost violently, vivid as a dream. She is bathed in sunlight. Her edges fade into the golden white nimbus that envelops her. In the glow, her dishevelled short afro appears to be ablaze. Her face is veiled in shadow. You cannot see it. You can never see it. She smells like camphor. You're small, very small, maybe two or three years old, you are not sure. She has seated you on a white plastic chair and she is kneeling in front of you, her back towards the window through which the dazzling bright light is gushing in. She is wearing a red dress. Her hand feels delicate and gentle as it takes your tiny foot and tickles it and you break out into a giggle. She laughs too as she carefully slides your foot into a little red and blue shoe but no sound comes out of her mouth. Only a shrill silence. You raise your small arms and try to reach for her face.

You are thrust forward as the bus comes to a jerky halt but your arms act just quickly enough to stop you from a painful collision with the seat in front of you. The little boy who is now kneeling in his mother's lap, is not so lucky. Biting your lower lip is all you can do to stop yourself from laughing as a shriek rips his mouth and jolts his mother awake. She looks more annoyed than sympathetic and throws him impatiently onto his rear on her lap. Sensing his mother's frustration and fearing any further admonishment, his cries quickly subside to sniffles and he pushes a thumb into his mouth. His little face is wet with tears.

Outside, the bus stop is lined with makeshift stalls, cardboards balanced on top of piles of rocks or bricks that serve as table legs. Each one is a slight iteration of the one next to it, displaying more or less the same assortment of snacks, fruits and vegetables. The vendors have already left their stands and started to besiege the bus, each trying to get as close to the windows as possible so the passengers can get a better view of their wares. They all chant what they are selling, attempting to sway prospective buyers by pointing out what is special about their particular product.

"Freezitsss. They are cold and frozen folks. Five bond only."

"Yes, mothers and fathers, I have your chips here. I have all the flavours: Lay's, Simbas, Spuds, Chompkins and Zap Naks. They are all here. Thirty bond only *vabereki*."

"Ehh bananas are over here. Seven for the big ones and five for the small ones. *Amai* buy some bananas for your child. Can you not see how hungry he looks? See, o he is even crying."

"My brother, do you want something to drink? All your drinks are here. Nice and cold they will properly cool your throat. The sun is very hot today, my brother."

After a while, you begin to detect a phantom rhythm in their discordance.

"*Mwanangu.*"

It is the tired woman. She is holding a dirty, five-dollar note, the edges eaten away from having gone through too many pockets and brassieres. You know the vendors will not accept it because it has 'Bond Note' written on the corner. They no longer accept such notes as valid currency. You say nothing.

"Can you buy some bananas for me?"

"How many?"

"I don't know. How ever much they can give you for that."

You turn towards the window and the moment they spot the money, the hawkers are drawn to you like flies. Baskets and card boxes and trays are pushed into your face. They chant even louder. None of them have bananas.

"I want bananas." Some of them seem disappointed. Others are angry and curse you under their breath. Regardless of their reaction, however, they all disperse immediately, almost as if it was choreographed, searching for other potential buyers.

A man who is just finishing transacting with a customer two windows away hears you and shouts that he is coming "faster faster," as soon as he finishes with his current customer. It is less for your benefit and more for any other vendors who might try to sell to you before he does.

When you hand him the bill, he pretends to examine it, but you know it is only a performance. He has already made up his mind. "Haa elder, what are you trying to do? Don't you know money like this does not work anymore?"

You start to turn to tell this to the woman, but in the end, you reach into your pocket and use your own money to buy two bananas.

As you are sitting down, something briefly catches your eye. You are uncertain what it is but it calls to you. It compels you. You scan the crowd of hawkers slowly. Your heart pounds the walls of your chest with a frenzied zeal. You can hear it thumping in your ears. Whatever it is you saw; it is demanding in its magnetism. The thing in your chest, it starts to swell again.

She is standing across the road, on the crack ridden pavement. She is tall and thin. There is an elegance to her slenderness. Her hands hang limply at her sides and her neck is bent at an odd angle. Her back is turned towards you but you know, in your bones you know it is her. She is wearing the red dress. There is a certain strangeness to the scene, an oddness that taunts you but lingers just beyond your reach. The harder you try to grasp what it is, the more it eludes you. The breeze gathers her camphor scent and carries it towards you. It feeds it into your nostrils and you clamour to breathe in every last bit of her. You immediately realise what the strangeness is. In spite of the wind, her dress hangs about her with an impossible stillness. In fact, everything about her has that same stillness, a quiet deadness.

The word begins to materialize in your mouth. You feel the weight of the syllables settle on your tongue before rolling on to your lips. It comes out as a whisper. Urgent. Needing. *Mhamha.*

She hears you. You are certain of it. She begins to turn to face you.

The engine coughs feebly before it sputters to life and then begins to roar. The distraction is only momentary. But even before you turn back, you know that she is gone.

***

When you disembark, Tariro is waiting for you at the bottle store. She is talking to some young man. When she sees you, a beaming smile adorns her plump face. She has gained some weight. The added layer of flesh accentuates the dimple on her left cheek. There is a new curvature to her body that was absent the last time you saw her. Her fashion sense has also changed noticeably. She is wearing a short, tight black skirt and a tank top that is a size or two too small so that the bottom part of her torso is not completely covered and her navel shows through. Strands of hair protrude stubbornly from the cornrows that line her head, suggesting the need for a touch up. Too much Vaseline endows her skin with a glossy sheen. The caveat, however, is that her slippered feet are now coated in a film of dust.

Her arms are already extended before she starts walking to come and give you a hug. She squeezes you tightly, and then stands back to get a better look at you and hugs you again.

"Brother. Is this you?"

Your smile is self-conscious. "Yes Tari. Who else could it be?"

"Mmm. Are you sure? The son of my mother, is this really you?"

"Stop playing games *kani.* Let us get my bags first."

"What did you bring for your sister, the village girl eh?"

"Just wait. You will see once we get home." Taking a more serious tone you ask her, "How is *Mbuya* Tandi?" You refer to your grandmother formally, using the family name, even though seven years have passed since you reunited with your maternal family.

"You will see once we get home." Her laugh is loud, easy and unburdened, a description that is equally true of her character.

She insists on carrying both your satchel and the *changani* bag that contains the few groceries you have brought. On the way, she tells you about the boy who has been chasing after her. The one she was talking to at the bottle store. She swears she wants nothing to do with him because she knows he only wants to get between her legs but you can tell, from the excitement in her voice and the glimmer in her eyes that she likely has already slept with him or is going to. You are used to your cousin's fibs. You find it amusing, her need to pass herself off as pristine, her tales often involving some form of temptation or other that she always manages to overcome. This girl, whose wardrobe suddenly runs out of loose-fitting clothes and whose buttocks inexplicably become more animated in the presence of men, she would have you believe that at twenty, she is still a virgin. Never mind that one of the boys she dated told you that he had slept with her. No, according to her, his propensity for lying borders on pathological and nothing he says is to be believed. On top of that he is also a crook, a womanizer, a drunk and all the people from his clan possess a malicious spirit that makes them ardent liars.

In spite of this, however, or maybe because of it, you enjoy her company. She makes you feel light, weightless. The thing in your chest that always accompanies you on your trips to your grandmother's feels restrained in her presence. It recoils against her carefreeness.

At midday, the sun sits in a cloudless sky with an apathy that is close to malice. The air is too dry, too stagnant, so much so that it is almost suffocating. It is late October, yet the rains have not yet come. All around you, the land is carpeted by a bleak brownness, dry, dull and dead: the trees, the grass, the shrubbery that forms a guard of honour along the dirt path that leads to your grandmother's homestead. With over a kilometre to go, the trek suddenly feels too long. Your temples start to throb, announcing the onset of a headache. The skin underneath your armpits is lathered in a sticky wetness. If not for the determination in Tariro's stride, you would find a tree to sit under and rest for a while. Half-heartedly you tell yourself that the sooner you get there, the better, and you trudge on.

You rush through greetings with your grandmother, eager to get to the object of your visit. Your replies to her inquiries about your health and that of those you have left in the city are brief. You wait the polite amount of time before you take your leave. You are at the door when she speaks. Her words seize you, stopping you mid-stride. "Must you keep doing this every time my child? What good can come of it?"

You have asked yourself the same question many times. As always, all your answers and justifications feel inadequate. You say nothing and walk away.

Tariro has just started plucking the feathers off a chicken when she sees you. "Should I come with you? I am almost finished here." Her voice is fraught with concern. She always asks you. Except for the first time, when you didn't know the way, your answer is always the same.

You do not face her. "No. I will be okay."

***

The grave lies in a disused field a short distance behind the homestead, lonely, its solemnity beckoning. Inside, your chest is running out of room. The plainness of the concrete gravestone is evidence of the reluctance with which it was constructed. Tariro told you the first time you visited. Your grandparents had been ashamed and had begrudgingly had the marker made only at her mother's insistence. After that, however, they refused to perform any of the ceremonies that usually follow a burial, the *nyaradzo* – the memorial service, and the *chenura* – the acquittal ceremony that ensures that the spirit of the deceased goes to the afterlife and is freed from all ties to the living world.

A handwritten inscription callously punctuates the end of your mother's life, summing her up, all that she was and all that she meant to the world, in three words.

Anastasia Tandi

Daughter, Wife, Mother

1972 – 2000

RIP

The slab and the entire area surrounding it is covered by the dry leaves of the *munhondo* tree that stands sentry about two meters to the right, its canopy sheltering the grave from the harsh glare of the mid-afternoon sun. The carpet of leaves crunches under your sneakers. A cock crows in the distance. The birds tweet their harmonies. All around you, life continues, the world is oblivious of you.

It is the same tree from which your mother was hanging the last time you saw her.

Even though it has been eroded by time, the sight is still etched into the foundation of your memory. The noose coiled around her neck. The peculiar angle at which her head hangs to the side. The red dress. Her eyes partially closed leaving only the whites visible through thin slits. Her body is still twitching. You peer at her curiously.

You do not understand the game that she is playing.

"*Mhamha?*" She does not answer. You sit at the foot of the tree and wait for her to stop playing and come down.

You do not understand why Aunty Felistus is screaming like that. Why she throws herself on the ground again and again. Why she picks you up so brusquely and carries you home, leaving your mother all by herself.

You do not understand why she calls out frantically for someone to come and help her. What does she need help with? You can help her with whatever it is.

You do not understand why your father who you have not seen for several months suddenly comes but you are happy that he does. His voice is stern and low when he talks to your grandparents. He does not enter their hut but speaks to them while standing outside. Occasionally, he gestures at you wildly and your grandparents lower their faces sombrely as if they have done something that they are not supposed to. After a while, Aunty Fiona comes out with your bag, the blue one with the drawings of puppies on it, and she puts it into your father's car. You drive away with your father, wondering if your mother has stopped playing her strange game yet.

You do not see Aunty Felistus or your grandparents for the next fourteen years. When Aunty Felistus messages you on Facebook you do not remember her. She is now called Mai Tariro. She hopes she can get a chance to meet you. Your father is upset but he allows you to visit her at her house in Warren Park.

You tell her you would like to see some pictures of your mother. You can see the sudden shifting in the features of her face. She tells you that your grandparents took them all and burned them. "They were ashamed, you see."

"Oh."

"But I have something. It is not much, but maybe it will help. It is mostly burnt though."

She hands you the charred remnant of a photo. Most of the top right corner is gone, along with the head of the slender woman that stands in it.

"I'm sorry, it is all I have."

"Can I see where she is buried?"

"Of course. I will take you there."

***

You sense her, even before she steps out from behind the trunk of the tree. As usual, your mother is facing away from you.

As your words try to rush out all at once, they stumble over each other, collecting into a bulging mass that catches in your throat.

In the end, one of them manages to escape. "Why?" It tumbles out of your mouth and sits on the ground between you and her, dense, laden with desperation.

Slowly, she turns to face you.

Inside your chest, everything bursts.

The Watch

Shingirai carefully turns the transparent plastic sleeve upside down and shakes it until the watch begins to slide out. It lands in the open palm of his left hand and he immediately notices its weight, how light it is. It feels cheap. When he bought the watch at Avondale Flea Market, he had been in a rush, so he hadn't noticed the lightness. He had just taken the first watch he saw that resembled the one he was looking for and paid the fifteen dollars for it without haggling for the price as he normally would have done. His heart sinks.

As he examines it more closely, he begins to notice other details, minute differences from his own. He frowns. He walks over to his wardrobe and slides open the drawer where he keeps his accessories, his collection of bracelets with the emblems of mainstream superheroes, his neck chains, rings and his glasses. He finds his watch at the back of the drawer and pulls it out. The lines on his forehead deepen. The face of his watch is slightly bigger than that of the one he had bought. The Alarm Chrono is spelt 'Chorno' on the watch from the flea market and Illuminator is spelt with an 'e' instead of 'o'. The 'I' in CASIO is also a lower-case font. He wipes it with his finger to make sure it isn't some speck on the letter. It isn't. He flips them both over. The text on the back is similar although the one on his original one is more deeply indented into the metal, which has a more metallic looking sheen to it than the plasticky material of the fake. He sighs and puts his watch back into the drawer and slides it shut.

He had certainly bought a fake. For the price, he could not have suspected that it was. He had bought his for the UAE dirham equivalent of twenty dollars in Dubai, and this one for only five dollars less. He had thought the price difference was because these kinds of old, classic watches were less popular in Zimbabwe where the current trend was bootleg versions of popular smartwatches and fitness bands. It had been hard to find the watch. He had gone to Joina City, Gulf Complex, Ximex Mall and Kwameh Mall and to every stall and corner shop he could find in the Harare CBD that sold electronics. And then he had finally asked Andrew, the man from whom he bought all his sneakers and caps who worked at Avondale Flea Market, who had finally directed him to this watch that he was already starting to regret having wasted his money on.

Shingirai's excitement about finally getting his father a birthday present for the first time was dissipating like dew under the morning sun. He had thought of the idea when his father saw his watch and commented how, back in his school days, they used to have watches just like that one, before jokingly asking him for it. That had been in January, when his father had asked him to accompany him on one of his trips to their plot in Goromonzi. He had forgotten about it until he saw the reminder on his phone that his father's birthday would be in two weeks. It would have been the perfect gift, yet now he found himself wondering whether he would even give his father the present. If he did, it would seem like he was being cheap, giving him the gift out of a sense of obligation rather than genuine affection. But maybe his father would not notice. He had nothing to compare it to. Even if he had owned one in secondary school, he certainly couldn't remember exactly what it had looked or felt like. Even Shingirai himself had been fooled and he had been wearing his own watch at the time he had made the purchase.

He tries to press the button at the top left corner of the watch that would turn on its lighting mechanism. The watch slips out of his hand and drops to the floor. When he picks it up, he notices that the digital face is slightly askew, diagonally slanted to the right at a small but noticeable angle. Had that been there before? He presses the light button and again and notices that the entire window containing the time and date moves as he does. He notices too, how the buttons feel soft and loose when he presses them. His father would certainly notice these things. He flings the watch against the wall.

There was no time to go and look for a replacement; the flea market would be closed by now and his father's birthday was tomorrow. He had wanted to give him the gift, first thing in the morning so it would not look like an afterthought. And who was to say that even if he did find a new one, it would not be a fake too. How could he have failed such a simple task? Perhaps his father had good cause to be as disappointed in him as he was. He was already twenty-five, unemployed, still living at home and with no clue what he wanted to do with his life. He had long since stopped applying for a master's degree after multiple rejections or only being accepted to small start-up universities that charged fees that were too high. He had only submitted one half-heartedly compiled CV since his graduation, for a graduate trainee position, to an NGO he could no longer remember the name of. They never emailed him back.

A few weeks ago, Shingirai's father had called him into the sitting room after everyone else had gone to bed and he had instantly known that something was wrong from the way he wore his face like stone, serious, stern, and dark under the dim lights in the room. He had been walking in after having spent the day at his cousins', drinking and playing video games on their brand new PlayStation 5. His father had asked him if he had eaten and he replied that he had not, but was not hungry. He was told to eat all the same and he had been too disturbed by the way his father was acting to argue. As he had his meal of sadza and mushrooms and chicken feet in a stew that had congealed, he tried to determine what it could be he had or hadn't done. He had washed the cars the previous day. He had cleaned out the garage as his father had instructed him to. He could not think of any chores he had forgotten to do. Maybe his father had found out about the twenty dollars change Shingirai had not given back to him when he had sent him to buy some new tools for the garage.

It had been a long time since his father had given him a lecture. After he finished picking at his meal, he deliberately cleared his throat to get his father's attention to announce that he had finished, but his father kept his eyes fixed on the Julius Caesar documentary that he was watching on the History channel. Eventually he had announced that he was finished and his father had only nodded but showed no signs that he was ready to start talking. Shingirai had waited, feeling like the criminals he saw in movies who were left to 'stew' in the interrogation room as a means to extract a confession. It was only when the end credits of the documentary were rolling that his father switched off the TV and turned to him.

"Do you know why I have called you here?"

Shingirai impishly smiled, the way he always did when someone was looking directly at him, even though he did not mean to. "No."

"Do you know that today is Father's Day?"

He knew that it was. "Really? I didn't know." It was another instance where the words that came from his mouth were not the ones he intended to say; they were the exact opposite in fact, which he did when he was nervous. The clothes on his body began to feel too small and hot.

That morning he had stood at the door to his parents' bedroom to tell them that he was about to leave to go to his cousins' house. He had intended to wish his father Happy Father's Day but could not decide how best to say the words. Any way that he thought of, any gesture, any inflection of tone, what combination of words he would use, sounded unnatural and forced. It was not something he was used to doing, not in person. Most of the previous Father's days had happened while he was at school and he could easily send a text message. In the end he had decided against saying anything at all and had ended up leaving without announcing his departure altogether.

"Of course, you didn't. These things are not important to you." The words wounded him, cut deep into his heart. "Anyway, it doesn't matter. Tell me, what is a father to you?"

The question caught him by surprise. Already feeling like an animal cornered, anxious and eager to escape, his mouth blurted out a response before he could allow himself time to think. "A father is a man who gives birth to a child…" His father's eyes remained fixed on him, he assumed, expecting more and he had to clench his jaw to keep himself from smiling again "…and cares for that child." He blinked, acutely conscious of the action, of his eyes, his face and body. His mouth felt dry and he could not find words. They sat in silence for a while.

"And that is all?"

Shingirai nodded, this time failing to resist his urge to smile. His father made a disgusted sound with his throat and Shingirai felt himself start to shrivel. "So, you, my son, are telling me that … ehhh … according to you, a father is just the man who fucked and impregnated your mother and gives you whatever you want?"

"No, Daddy. That's not…"

"Isn't that what you just said?"

"Yes, but…"

"Then why are you saying it is not? *Handiti* that is what you said, yes?"

Shingirai hung his head and mumbled under his breath, "Yes."

"So that is all I am to you?" He was shocked to hear the sadness in his father's voice, the cadence of it that of someone about to cry – not just cry, but grieve.

"I didn't mean … A father also supports and guides their son through life. And…" Again, there are no words.

"So, you only measure a father by what he can do for *you*? Never mind how he feels or what he needs. A father is just like an ATM machine, you just press it and get whatever you want." His father exhaled, the irregular, shuddering way one would when they had just been crying or a chill had gone through them.

Shingirai said the only thing he knew to, when he did not know what else to say, "Sorry, Daddy."

"My father, for all his faults, was the greatest man I ever knew. It's a shame you never got to know him, the real him. You only saw him after he was old and he was this grumpy old man to you. You probably wondered why we bothered going to see him every school holiday like we did, didn't you?" Shingirai opened his mouth, about to stammer a response, still assessing in his head whether he had actually liked his grandfather, but his father did not wait to hear his response. "But to me, he was the best man I have ever known. He was wise, he had compassion and he was always there when I needed him." His father reached into his pocket and pulled out his handkerchief. He tentatively pulled his glasses from his face and wiped them before wiping his eyes and sliding them back on. As he did this, Shingirai stared at the TV, at its shiny surface, a black rectangle in which other versions of them were having the same conversation. Or maybe it was different in there. Maybe in there, his father's words did not make him feel the way he now felt. Incomplete. Maybe the father in there was telling his son how proud he was of the man he'd become, how much he appreciated him.

"I remember how I used to talk to my old man during those holidays when we visited. I don't think you and I have ever talked like that. I wonder why that is."

All Shingirai could say was, "Sorry Daddy."

"It's fine." His father nodded slowly and then repeated, "It's fine."

Shingirai hears those words again as he examines the watch. He feels the burden of them, and he wishes he could sink. That conversation had stayed with him for days afterwards, more painful each time he thought about it, drawing a cloud around him in which there were all of his insecurities, his inadequacies, fears and lack of worth.

Nothing was fine.

He takes one last look at the watch, puts it back into the sleeve and puts it in his drawer, next to his.

A Hole in the Air

I wish Sekuru would die already.

I'm not sorry for what the majority of you, in your self-aggrandisement, will no doubt consider my callousness. Maybe my personality can be regarded as crude, lacking a certain refinement that makes it more agreeable, but I would hardly call myself unsympathetic.

The days prior to Sekuru's illness, my brother Tonde had got into the habit of waking up at five-thirty in the morning and going jogging. "Six kilometres," he often bragged even though I had looked the distance up on the map and it was just a little over five kilometres. He would come back sweaty and thirsty, his hairy thighs and calves glistening and bulging below his running shorts. He would go straight to the refrigerator, often leaving sweat stains on the handles that I had to wipe. After gulping down two tumblers of brain freezing water, he would march to our backyard and do thirty repetitions of pull ups on the swing set that was there. He finished off his morning routine with thirty to forty minutes of callisthenic exercises and stretches on a yoga mat in his bedroom, concluded by a hot bath. He often left puddles of soapy water on the bathroom floor and inside the bathtub which, I again, had to clean up.

The morning after we learned that Sekuru was ill, he did not go jogging. He did not leave stains on the fridge or in the tub. In fact, he did not leave his room until it was time for breakfast. Even then, he did not hungrily devour the food like a starved hyena the way he usually did. He picked at it and hardly nibbled at his sweet potatoes before silently leaving the dinner table. I looked at Daddy. And then at

Mhamha. Their eyes were fixed on their plates with the concentration of one who feared that if they looked away even for a moment, their food would be stolen. None of them seemed to care that Tonde had left before we clapped our hands.

It was Sekuru who introduced the custom of clapping our hands after meals. One day after supper, when he had come to visit us, he cleared his throat and said, "We should thank our ancestors and our Creator who have given us this food and the life so that we may be able to enjoy this meal together. And also thank the people who work hard every day to put this food before us. I do not know, am I mistaken?" Whenever he ended a speech by asking that question, it meant you were not supposed to disagree with him. He looked around and in the way that he often did, took our silence as agreement. Then he and Daddy proceeded to clap in the traditional way of us Manyika people. The males go first. They cup their hands and then clap them together seven or eight times in quick succession, then there is a brief pause proceeded by three slower claps. Then the women follow, their hands cupped as well, but they clap them perpendicular to each other, and continue to do so until all thanks have been said or all greetings have been exchanged. After Sekuru left, Daddy carried on with the custom and no one was allowed to leave the dining table until we had clapped our hands.

That morning, I watched silently as Tonde went to his room and slammed the door shut. Daddy and Mhamha's eyes remained on their plates.

Even though Daddy's love for Sekuru has all the restraints of fearful respect that is almost prerequisite in traditional father-son relationships, it is still quite apparent. My father is the first of two sons in a family of five and therefore, by default, Sekuru's favourite. Even though he is the second born, growing up, he often enjoyed all the benefits of being the first, a condition which has made my eldest aunt estranged from him and the rest of the family. Out of all his children's families, Sekuru visits us the most and stays the longest. We all know it is more than him simply not wanting to spend too much time living with his sons-in-law, or our uncle, whom he claims drinks too much.

This favouritism extends to Tonde, my brother who also has the added benefit of being Sekuru's namesake and the older one between the two of us. Saying that I live in his shadow in the eyes of our grandfather would be a misstatement. No, my brother individually occupies the spaces that are meant for the both of us.

I felt the effects of this partiality the most during the year that we stayed in the village with our grandparents and the holidays we visited them at the end of every school term. Especially during the rainy season when Sekuru used to go to work in the fields. When he came back from the farm, he often brought gifts for his grandson. *Hwiza*, small birds, *mbewa, magurwe* or the first ripe maize after the ploughing season which is *my* favourite. He would always give them to Tonde and then ask him to share the food with me, a request which, more than anything, felt like a grudging courtesy rather than genuine affection. I suspect too, that it was at the insistence of my grandmother. May she rest in peace. I lived in a dimension of my own, a cold and unkind elsewhere, and

I still bear the scars to show for it. Those scars started itching and bleeding anew after Sekuru became ill.

I called it the season of last breaths – the period just before Sekuru got sick. There were four funerals in the space of a fortnight: My grandmother's brother, Sekuru's nephew, an uncle whose relation to us was obscure and distant and finally, my grandmother. Even the fact that all the deceased were above sixty, the average life expectancy in Zimbabwe, the closeness of their deaths still raised a fair amount of eyebrows and featured prominently on the grapevine.

My parents attended all the funerals. I think it was the third funeral. Or was it the second? To me, they all eventually conflated into one long stretch of silent meals, absent parents and calls from relatives offering their condolences. But I'm certain it wasn't the last one, my grandmother's, because we all went for that one. So, while my parents were away for the second or third funeral, Tonde brought his girlfriend home to stay overnight. I sensibly expressed my disapproval by spitting in their food. But in typical fashion whenever Tonde and I are at odds with one another, I ended up being the one disappointed. They never ate the food.

That was the first time that my brother snuck his girlfriend into the house. The second time he brought her home, my parents had gone to the village after receiving the news of Sekuru's illness. My room is adjacent to his, separated by one particularly thin wall, and I've watched my fair share of porn – strictly for educational purposes – to deduce that my brother is quite proficient in bed. Either that or his girlfriend is very enthusiastic in prayer and really approves of whatever it is God is doing for her and wants

Him to keep doing it just like that. Still, I know enough to realise that the sounds I heard weren't sex. Someone was crying. Sad crying, not the sexy kind. Sniffles, snot and tears. I could hear the girl whispering her consolation and I imagined my brother, with all his bulging muscles, curled up in a foetal position with his head on the girl's lap, eyes red and watery, his nose running, as she stroked his head and tried – and failed – to convince him that everything was going to be ok. Then she would slide her hand into his shorts and stroke him there as well.

Given what had happened over the past two weeks, our reaction to the news of Sekuru's illness was not incomprehensible. Nonetheless, knowing this did little to ease its effects on our household, to lighten the gloom that infested every corner of our house like mould. It crept in from the fringes of our home, steadily consuming everyone and everything inside.

Tonde has stopped running altogether. He has stopped eating. He is usually the most vibrant member of our family, and the diminishing of his bright persona has left us all in a dark and heavy shadow. He retreats into his bedroom and then into himself. In fact, the only evidence of his presence anymore is the sound of the loud music that he plays to drown out the sound of his crying.

Then there's Daddy. Like my brother, he chose a prison of his own to contain his grief. For him it is his home office. Mhamha asked me to not call him for mealtimes anymore. She carries his food to him herself. I see him only when he comes for supper, his laptop bag sagging from his shoulder as if he carries the full weight of his despair in there. Always the conversationalist, but he has dwindled down to monosyllabic responses and only uses full sentences where it is absolutely unavoidable. The few times that he does talk he reminisces about the days of his youth and the adventures that he went on with his father: climbing mountains to collect *mazhanje*; crossing overflowing rivers; going on long journeys teeming with adventure. You can tell that he is lost in that past world that has faded to sepia with time and wishes he could revisit it if only for a moment of reprieve. It is a world that has its share of regrets, dreams and missed opportunities. But most importantly, it is a world where he has his father, happy and healthy.

It is more than just sentiment that eats at Daddy, that chases the sleep from his bloodshot eyes in the night and makes him walk about like a lost soul with an invisible burden on his back. There are also the financial repercussions. Daddy chose one of the best hospitals for Sekuru's treatment and the most highly regarded geriatrician. He had to. For the optics more than anything else. He understandably does not want to give his siblings something to talk about. I disagree with the idea, but I understand. Of course, he will never admit it, but it is there in his eyes. The look of exasperation that glazes them whenever he hands more money to the lady at the hospital reception with the store bought, perpetual smile. The minute frown when he sits at the dining table and sees the cabbage or the dried vegetables on his plate.

Mhamha is not as aggrieved. She is only saddened to the extent that is expected of her as a wife and a daughter-in-law. Sometimes she is uncharacteristically curt with me and wont to sudden bursts of anger. That is the extent of it. As a wife she could not help falling a little under the shadow of the dark cloud that hangs over her husband.

We visited Sekuru yesterday.

It was Sunday. For the first time since I graduated high school I went to church. We all did. The last time we did so as a family was maybe when I was still in primary school. Even then, it was only so I could clock in enough hours in Sunday school to be baptised and be able to gain admission at St. Dominic's, a catholic mission school that my parents were insistent that I attend. But yesterday we all did. The ride, like every other family event these days, was silent. I imagined each person was doing their best to suppress the same thought that I had: Sekuru was better off dead. This sudden need to commune with the almighty was nothing more than a desperate effort at repentance for this sinful thought. Or maybe it was just me. The service was "beautiful." The sermon was "powerful." And the singing was "angelic." We went home, fat with the Holy Spirit, and looking forward to how it would repay us for the forty dollars that we had so generously given to the church. I hear God works in his own time, so I was not too discouraged that everything felt the same as we drove back home.

At the hospital, Sekuru looked a remnant of the man in Daddy's sepia world. Bursts of violent coughs threatened to disintegrate what little was left of him. His rheumy eyes could barely stay open and each time they remained shut for too long, anxious glances shot across the room. The air in the small wardroom was thick with something unspoken; something opaque yet intangible that filled the gaping holes inside all of us.

Boys

Getting off the *kombi*, Nigel's nose is instantly assailed by the fetid aroma of a burst sewer blended with the ripe fragrance of some decaying animal. A mound of partially burnt trash lies casually in the drain that runs along the side of the pothole ridden main road, the flattened carcass of a dog that has been run over by a car splayed ornamentally on top of it like the cherry on top of a garbage sundae.

Around him, the familiar dissonant voices of Glen Norah pervade the hot September afternoon; dusty children chasing each other around and laughing, resonant with juvenile ignorance; a troop of young men calling out to each other while their sweaty bodies glisten in the sun as they play a game of seven aside on a patch of land where the grass has long since given way to rocky ground; a cluster of girls talking in low murmurs as they stand in a queue at the water pump, exchanging gossip, with their buckets sitting next to them like obedient children; a car parked in front of one of the flats with loud music spilling out of its open doors. The song is 'Ndaremerwa' by Holy Ten:

> *"…Cash talk mahwambi pa town*
>
> *These days hazvina kumira mushe*
>
> *Graduate rahwandisa gown*
>
> *Ndoyacho hazvidi kuti apuse…"*

The afternoon is lazy, tepid. Eager to escape the stench that has now settled at the back of his mouth and started coiling itself around his uvula, he darts into Zambezi Close, the side street that leads towards the flats. The conductor of the *kombi* that he has just disembarked hits it on the side with the palm of his hand and it roars away, the cry of its horn trailing behind it through the air.

An indifferent sun watches the scene from a cloudless sky, watches the young man with a mop of thumb long, stringy dreadlocks trudge slowly down the street where scabby patches of asphalt tell the long-forgotten tale of better times, escorted disconsolately by his thoughts and the lifeless air that is replete with summer mid-afternoon languor.

Nigel winces, the pain in his jaw shooting up the side of his face and stinging his eyes. He runs a dry tongue over his torn lower lip. His father's voice comes from some distant place inside of him, rumbling and commanding, *Men do not cry.* With a violent suddenness, a surge of emotions erupts within him that he grips desperately in his clenched fists. A tormented scream rises from the floor of his stomach and into his throat, only to shatter into a tarnished silence on his tongue.

He cannot free himself of his father even now. He is still haunted by him, a phantom rooted within the depths of his emotions. It is watchful of his every thought with a severe, judgmental gaze.

"Nijo!" He swivels around, losing his balance for a moment.

There is a woman sitting behind her kiosk under the shade of one of the few trees that still dot the length of the street, a leafless, skeletal *Musau* tree that no longer bears fruit, from which an orange reflective vest with the Econet logo hangs tiredly. A baby is fastened to her back, secured by a threadbare wrapper, alarmingly still, and from that distance, could well be dead. The woman does not acknowledge the fat green fly buzzing around her head, her glazed eyes fixed on something in the distance, in the future.

"Hey Nijo! Over here."

His eyes follow the voice to a dusty, dark skinned boy standing at the edge of the pitch where the young men are playing their game, waving his arms enthusiastically. The boy has the long limbs and elongated frame of a pubescent child. Stinkz. *Shit!*

Nigel forces his mouth to form the taut, vague shape of a smile and waves back only to immediately regret it when the boy takes this as an invitation and starts walking toward him.

Nhamo 'Stinkz' Boora, was one of the local Robins who lived around the flats. A Robin was a boy who preferred the company of more senior boys to that of his contemporaries. Robins were convenient to have when you needed someone to send on errands; someone to go buy some beer at the shops or get a message to a girl if there had been no electricity for too long and you were unable to charge your phone. They were especially essential when you had been smoking ganja and needed to get some more, but were too high to go to the dealer yourself. For this, Stinkz was very good. He never took a cut for himself like most of the other boys did. He had asthma. But Stinkz had two problems. The first was that he could not stop talking. Once you started a conversation with him, he would go on and on, windy monologues riddled with repetition and peppered with fallacies. And even when you tried to give him a hint that you had had enough or you were simply not in the mood for talking, that would only get him to change the subject. His verbosity was handy at times. He knew, and spared no expense sharing, everything that went on around the flats, around all of Glen Norah; who was dating who, who had stolen from where and who had got beaten up at the nightclub the previous night. From Machipisa to Chitubu, if it happened, he would tell you. The second problem, and what earned him his nickname, was that he smelled. He always carried about him the stench of dirty wet socks that had been worn too long on a hot day. Even after taking a bath and dousing himself with deodorant, the stale odour would still cling about him like moss to a damp wall. And the smell was at its worst when he was sweating, which he was now, having just come off the pitch.

Anxious to avoid the smell, Nigel quickens his pace and points at his wrist to indicate that he was in a hurry, turning away before the boy has a chance to respond.

A gateless entrance leads into the car park of the apartment complex where Kudakwashe, his childhood friend, lives with his mother. Their flat is on the topmost of three storeys of a worn apartment building where the staircase has started to show a series of dangerous looking cracks and the railing on one side of it has fallen off. A column that stands in the centre of the concourse, supporting the network of landings, nests a beehive and is covered in bird shit. The pigeons that have daubed this faecal design line the edge of the roof, cooing nonchalantly. Nigel knocks twice before there is a response.

The door is opened by Kudakwashe's mother, a clammy, stout and neckless woman with an ever-present frown and disproportionately thin legs that look like spare parts attached to her body. What Nigel would call chicken legs when he was teasing his friend. She pants as she stands in the doorway. Her greeting is a further deepening of the lines on her forehead before she calls for her son.

"Kudaa! *Iwe* Kudakwashe!"

"*Mhaa!*" A voice echoes from the dinginess of the dim hallway.

She waddles back into the apartment, leaving the door open without inviting Nigel in. Her son emerges a few moments later wearing nothing but a pair of checked boxer shorts, a tall, slender young man with the shifty eyes of a swindler and an almost handsome face were it not for the plague of lumpy, puss tipped acne that covers it.

Seeing his friend at the door, his eyes light up. "Ah Nijo, *madii?*"

"King, how's it going?"

"*Haa bho.* It's all good. I was thinking it was somebody that I owe money. I was not expecting you this early. Everything good?"

"Yes. Get dressed."

"You want to go now?"

"Yes. Is that a problem?"

"*Maya. Isusu* we can hit it twenty-four-seven you know that. From dawn till dusk. Pressure zero *baba*."

"Hurry up then." Nigel feels increasingly impatient with his friend who he thought had a penchant for always using more words than were necessary, a trait he did not presently appreciate.

Kudakwashe grins and puts a hand on Nigel's shoulder. "This is the problem with you Nijo. You are too fast man. You should keep calm, like us, your elders. *Inga wani* the bible says patience is a virtual."

Nigel sighs. "Virtue."

"Huh?"

"Patience is a virtue. Not virtual." He had learned that from his cousin who spoke English like it was drinking water.

"*Wangu,* this does not get you girls. Let me get dressed *apa.*"

Kudakwashe disappears back into the flat and is replaced a few seconds later by the voice of his mother in the open doorway. "Where are you going Kuda?"

"Out."

"Out where?"

Silence.

"To do what?"

"Nothing."

"Of course you are. Instead of getting a job like a responsible adult you are just wasting time doing god knows what with that good for nothing crook. Is this how you want to repay me for sending you to university?"

"*Mhamha* don't start again with that."

"Don't start what? Did I ever finish? *Handiti* you always run away whenever I try to talk to you."

"I need to get going."

"You think because you have that beard that makes you look like a goat you are now too grown up to listen to me *eh*? You think you are a man? Is that so? If your father was here would you be acting like this?"

"Well then, maybe you should have done a better job of keeping him."

The end of the conversation is sharply punctuated by the sudden bang of a door slamming shut.

It is not the first time Nigel had heard his friend fighting with his mother. Their arguments are frequent, even more so since Kudakwashe's father had announced, almost a decade ago, that he would be marrying another woman in South Africa where he was working.

Kudakwashe reappears in the doorway, now dressed. A smudge of the latest ointment he was applying to his face to help with the acne is still smeared on his chin.

"Do you have the stuff?" Nigel asks as they descend the stairs. He could use something to calm his mind which had been tormenting him all day. Since morning, it had been sifting through his life with tiringly dogged determination, lingering on the worst parts of his past and present, stretching them out and filling him with dread for the future that made him feel as if he was trapped underwater.

"No, I had not yet gone to buy. I was not expecting you this early, you know."

"*Haa* so *pakaipa* because I need something faster faster. I have been doing rounds since morning and I just need something, you understand?" Nigel looks forlornly into the distance, already feeling his thoughts rearing their heads, ugly as sin.

"Hoo, when you are out hustling you do not invite us but then when we start doing our own things you want to be featured. But it's not cool man."

"It's not like that King."

"So what were you doing?"

"I was looking for a house."

"House? Why? You do not want to stay at home anymore?"

Nigel does not respond. His mind begins to replay the events of the previous night. Kudakwashe's voice is lost in the downpour of the foggy memory.

His father had finally kicked him out of the house. It was an anticlimactic conclusion in its expectedness, having been presaged by each fight between father and son over the years, each reproach that fell on deaf ears, each time he did yet another thing that angered his father and made his mother cry. He was having a hard time remembering most of it. What he did recall was the stench of vomit and alcohol, his head spinning and the taste of blood.

He had arrived home sometime in the middle of the night, too drunk to know what time it was, the only indicator of his lateness being that the doors were all locked. After banging on the window to his parent's window for a while, a face finally peered through the curtains. He could not tell whose it was, his mother's or father's. It must have been his father because he was the one that finally opened the door for him. There were some words spoken that he could not hear, but they must have been angry because his father's eyes were red and his forehead sported a million folds. He had said something back. Something funny. He was laughing. And then the blood, metallic in his mouth. A dull pain on his jaw. His father on the kitchen floor, clutching his stomach and trying to burn a hole through him with his eyes. The dryness in his throat echoed faintly a memory of him heaving and spraying his father with partially digested chunks of meat swimming in a pool of Zambezi beer. But through all of it, one memory in particular stood out, starkly clear; the sound of his father's voice as he disappeared down the corridor that led to his bedroom. "You are no son of mine. I do not want to see you in this house tomorrow morning"

Kudakwashe is talking, "…fucking woman will not get off my case about getting a job."

"Sorry, what?"

"My mom. She just will not stop with her bullshit. *Hee* Kuda get a job, *hee* I sent you to varsity. Kuda this, Kuda that. Fuck *mhani*."

"But you have a job."

"Apparently not according to her. If it does not have a salary then it is not a job."

"*Wangu*, our parents do not understand that things have changed. You cannot just finish form four and become a teacher anymore."

"You know?"

"Why don't you try applying for those road construction jobs? I heard E.D. invested some serious bag for fixing our roads this year. I am sure they are hiring. Even a dropout should not have a problem getting that."

"*Haa* you know you can never trust these kinds of stories nowadays. Are you forgetting the time they said they were going to fix the electricity issue those days? You could wake up tomorrow morning and hear that all the money was stolen. And even if I wanted to *ka*, those jobs are basically slavery. You only get enough money to afford transport to go there and back and to buy a packet of *maputi* for lunch only. No man, I will stick to selling second hand clothes. At least I can save a little something and afford ganja. By the way, don't you want some jeans Nijo? I have them very cheap."

Nigel looks at his friend for a moment. His attempt at laughter fails to be anything more than a weak half-smile that fades as quickly as it appears.

"*Mudhara* my pants hanging at my waist like this is not by choice. It is because I am too skinny and I was given these pants by my cousin who lives uptown. They used to fit but poverty has been eating me."

"*Pakaipa* my guy. You used to be very muscular. I was not even afraid to provoke people on the streets when I was with you. But now *eh*."

"Tell me about it."

They arrive at the car playing the Zim dancehall music. Jeffrey 'Fuje' Masango, the local drug peddler is sitting inside. From the way he is dressed; a pair of ripped jeans through which a hairy thigh can be seen on one leg and a blackened knee on the other, a bootleg golden Rolex studded with fake diamonds around the rim of the watch-face, and a cap facing backward meant more to cover his balding head than anything else, most people do not realise that he is already on the wrong side of forty. All that gives a hint of his age is a protuberant paunch that is stuffed under his Chelsea jersey. There is a girl sitting in the passenger's seat that Nigel recognises but whose name he cannot recall.

"Hi Tracy. Fuje *madii*."

Tracy lives in the apartment opposite Kudakwashe's. Nigel recalls hearing a rumour from Stinkz that she was pregnant.

Fuje's irritation is poorly concealed when he answers. "King, how far? Nijo, all good?"

Nigel nods his head but opts to let his friend do the talking. "Low low. Sorry for disturbing you two love birds."

Tracy scowls and clicks her tongue. "It's ok, you are not disturbing anything. I was just leaving."

Fuje looks at the two younger men, weighing losing his pride against potentially not getting the thing he had been after the entire time he had been with his girlfriend. He turns to her, "Tracy don't be like that baby."

"*Hmm hmm*. Don't be like that *chii chacho*. I told you to take me to town but you said let's stay here what what. We can make it work, you said. How many people have come while we were sitting here? *Ipapa* I am dying of hunger and you did not even at least buy me some food. Not even a packet of Zap Naks or a bottle of Pepsi. What kind of a man is so stingy?"

"But baby you know I need to work. Things are tough and this is the only way I can get money to take you out."

"Out? Out where? Have you ever taken me out? You think taking me to Chicken Inn and buying me a two piecer is taking me out? I do not have time for this, I am leaving. Look for me when you are serious and know how to treat a woman, do you hear me." She steps out of the car and slams the door shut. She is a few yards away when she realises that she has forgotten something and returns. Clicking her tongue intermittently, she opens the door, grabs her phone from the dashboard and slams the door once more before walking away. Nigel and Kudakwashe watch silently.

Deciding that any further grovelling would not be worth it, at least for the time being, Fuje shouts after her. "Go! I do not have time for whores like you." In a much lower voice he adds, "*Nhai* why should I waste my time pleading with a gold digger like that?" But the words lack any real conviction. He would, in fact, find time to plead with her, later, his pride shielded by the shelter of privacy.

"*Jahman* she is not worth it. Everyone knows that one is public property. Even I have eaten from that." While it was true that Tracy had dated a fair share of the boys who lived around the flats, Kudakwashe, in spite of his best efforts, was not one of them. She had taken one look at the acne on his face and laughed him off and he still hated her for it.

The three of them watch Tracy walk away, rolling her buttocks and swaying her hips in a manner that was clearly deliberate, meant to make a statement: look at what you are missing out on. It was not only a tease for Fuje, but also an open invitation to any other boys that were looking on.

Fuje ignores Kudakwashe's comment. "What do you boys want?"

"Personally, I want money and pussy but you do not have either, so just give us the usual."

Fuje sighs and extends his palm. Kudakwashe scoffs. "*Haa* Fuje just give us the goods and we will pay you. All those times that we come here, have we ever failed to pay you?" Fuje responds by rubbing his index and middle finger against his thumb. Kudakwashe grumblingly shoves his hand into his pocket and pulls out the money. He crumples the notes into a ball before throwing them onto Fuje's lap.

Sighing again, Fuje steps out of the car and walks over to the passenger side. He disappears briefly and when he resurfaces, he is holding a small plastic bag which he throws at no one in particular. "Now fuck off."

Kudakwashe grins. "Chillspot how far?"

"There is no one there. No one else comes this early in the day."

Nigel and Kudakwashe walk to the back of the flat where there is an old sofa covered by a black plastic sheet where several phallic symbols have been drawn into the dust that coats its surface.

Kudakwashe peels the sheet off and finds a rock to keep it in place. Both of them choose to sit on the arm rests of the sofa instead of on the mouldy seats. Nigel is the designated blunt roller because the one time Kudakwashe had tried to do so, he had spilled so much of it and put too much spit on the wrapping paper. Nigel goes about doing the job very slowly and deliberately, the way a man who had been wandering in the desert would drink the dew off a leaf. After he finishes, he pulls out a matchbox from his satchel, one of the few things he had managed to take with him before he left that morning, together with a few clothes. He lights the blunt and takes the first puff. He savours the taste of the ganja gathering around his tongue, its stench settling in his nose and feels the tears sting his eyes. He sees his father again through the curtain of smoke, on the floor.

Men do not cry.

A pair of hate filled eyes.

No son of mine.

Blood and vomit.

Good for nothing crook.

A door slams shut.

Too grown up to listen.

Kudakwashe takes his turn and leans against the wall. "So did you find it?"

"What?"

"The house."

"No."

Kudakwashe takes another puff and hands the blunt to Nigel. "So what are you going to do?"

Nigel looks up at the sky and studies the sun for a long while. He takes a drag. A swirl of smoke flows out of his mouth and rises, fading into the day and the noise.

"I have no idea."

Yesterday's Colours

Let's call her Noma. She smiles like eternal sunshine.

I'm not much for talking. I prefer living inside myself, wandering the dim hallways, sweeping the dust off of my past and tenderly caressing its rough surfaces. You can also probably tell that I'm a little dramatic. Ok, a lot dramatic. It's cool though. It's how I'm able to deliver such well written narratives. Oh yeah … I also have a bit of an ego, as you'll no doubt see a few times as you continue reading.

It was maybe six years ago. Or was it seven? It doesn't really matter, but it was quite a while back. She went to the same school as my cousin. So this cousin of mine had a crush on her. Even though he was a form behind her and he was two years her junior. So was I. Well I still am, it's not like I caught up to her. Fun fact: She and I share a birthday. Cool, right? Some written in the stars type shit.

My cousin … Let's give him a name too, say, Victor. Victor didn't have a phone then. I did. I was staying at my aunt's at the time, for reasons which may or may not become apparent further along in our story. So Victor got Noma's number at school. He's a ladies' man. By his own account, a compilation of his dating portfolio and sexual conquests boasts more than fifty girls, with degrees of class that span the entire spectrum from the ghettos of Glen View all the way to the affluent suburbs of Borrowdale. It's up to you whether or not you choose to believe him. But that's now. He wasn't quite as prolific six (or seven) years ago. Me, on the other hand … How can I put it? I've dated two girls in the last seven years. I've only slept with one of them. I was president of what was called the Nard Committee back in high school. Nard is what we called guys who were too scared to talk to girls. I was the goddamn president. Of course, Victor didn't know any of this. Nobody beyond the borders of my school did. I considered asking him to teach me the art of… fuck, I don't know. Just whatever would get me out of that fucking committee. But like I said, I have an ego. Besides, there's just something debasing in admitting to another man that you're not man enough. We were only boys then, but I've found that this is true regardless of age.

They talked on my phone, flirted even, but as far as I know, that was the extent of it. Noma later told me she wasn't interested in dating someone younger than her. Because girls-wise, my inventory was embarrassingly lacking, when Noma texted me one day, about a year later, trying to get in touch with Victor, well, I saw an opportunity. This was especially easy for two reasons. The first is, I was dating my first girlfriend back then, a relationship that lasted all of a month without us ever meeting for the entirety of its duration, coming to its anticlimactic conclusion when I was unable to send her a Valentine's Day gift because I really had no money, but she wouldn't believe me. We met on Facebook, this girl and I. Bite me. But it meant I didn't try as hard to impress Noma. I'm not very good at that. I don't know what girls want to hear. I know no man does, but my inability is beyond extraordinary. Two; I was about to leave the country to go and study abroad, so in the likely eventuality that our interaction took an unfortunate turn, then I could simply flee, change my number and leave her as just another old book on the dusty shelves of my memory. At worst, she would become something to flinch at when I happened to revisit that particular period in my life. Thankfully, it never came to that.

In spite of a clear disparity in the scopes of our respective intellects – mine significantly beyond hers – I was pleasantly surprised that I could stand talking to her and completely fucking thrilled that she enjoyed talking to me. Our initial conversations lacked the awkwardness that I'd become accustomed to whenever I tried to befriend a new girl. She was friendly, chatty, witty and dare I say, seemed to understand me, at least more than I expected her to. I could forgive a few of my witticisms going unappreciated. It was an instant vibe.

Here's something else you should know: She was the first girl I ever spoke to on a phone call. Before her, the only way I was able to communicate with girls was through text and even then, every word was obsessively overthought, each emoji painstakingly picked out and each reply studiously overanalysed. Anyway, by the time our friendship began to get into its stride, I'd already left Zimbabwe for China, so we didn't get a chance to meet in person. Which was probably for the better because I hit a growth spurt sometime in my late teens and early twenties which made me the viable prospect that I was for her – and any other single ladies out there – when I finally came back. During my time away, we talked A LOT. And while I was unused to that kind of attention, I'm no idiot. I correctly interpreted her actions as an interest in yours truly. The only problem: I was nine thousand nine hundred and fifty-five kilometres away (or fifty-seven depending on your source). Let me be clear, this wasn't a problem for me. My entire dating record was abridged by a month long relationship with a possible catfish.

It took me three years to shoot my shot.

Her heart was made of glass and I wanted nothing more than to steal it and put it on a velvet cushion and just surround it with lasers made of love. Always the poet, I am. When I eventually managed to salvage enough confidence to fill up my ball sack and tell her how I felt, I was a year late. Because of this walking, breathing scarecrow made from turds, jizz and … and fucking ugly toenails. Those kinds that make you wear socks with your slippers. You know those guys? The ones that find the perfect girl and then once she's spread her legs (or bent over because let's face it, missionary is for your mum and dad) they just treat her like a used tampon. Just keep it long enough to find an appropriate time to throw it away. The type that gives the rest of us men a bad rep. The dogs. That was this guy for you. Let's call him Sean. I always thought it sounded like a douchebag's name. Sean. Heh. Sean the douchebag.

It was so cliché. Proverbial even. She was a naïve virgin. She fell for him. She trusted him. He took advantage of her vulnerability and then betrayed her. When she told me about it, her voice was brimming with emotion. I knew she still suffered the hurt that he caused her and more than being discouraged by her rejection of my advances, I only wanted to console her. I wanted to let her know that not every guy is a Sean. I wanted to be the knight in shining armour that ventured into the void of her broken heart and recovered her faith in love. There's a certain kind of pleasure in fixing broken things that you can't find doing anything else. Loving a broken person is like passing that feeling through an amplifier.

A year passed. I graduated. Top of my class. Not that that's relevant, I just like letting people know. We stayed in touch and I nursed her wounds. I dressed them with the kind of attention that so many of us crave but dare not admit. I anointed them with assurances of a less disappointing tomorrow and in time I was able to wash out the bitter taste of betrayal from her mouth. The stale aftertaste of Sean's cum. Then it was time for me to come home.

Having been rejected once, I was understandably reluctant to venture again into the unpredictable terrain of courtship. In any case, I had exhausted the entire arsenal that I had in my testicles with the first attempt and my confidence had been shaken by that particular misadventure. But when it's meant to be, it will.

Our pieces were a perfect fit and not even my being a pussy could stop them coming together. We were meant for each other. There is something about just gradually easing into a partnership. It means you're so right for each other that, without any unnerving verbal transactions, you simply see it for yourselves and embrace it. There is no clear distinction between the time you were and weren't together but rather, you sort of just fade into each other. Your singular future absorbs your separate pasts and you can't recall a time when your paths weren't one. That's what we were. And my god, it was fucking euphoric.

The first time I saw her, six (or seven) years after we started talking, the first time I saw her smile, I wrote this poem for her:

You are beautiful.

Your honeyed smile is aglow with all the majesty of a diamond studded sky adorned by a vibrant silver moon.

When I muster the courage and look into the depths of your eyes, I feel infinite. I am seen, forever.

Time stretches and shudders at your touch. I am transcended. Transported. Lost in euphoric oblivion.

Your cheeks, supplely full and smoothly rounded to near perfect semi-spheres, rise when your luscious lips stretch into a glistening smile whose glow feels like the sunrise on my skin.

When you laugh I am alight, afire. I am.

The curves that define you are sublime and elegant and, in their embrace, I lose myself.

When I trace a quivering hand over them, my heart dances to the song of an autumn breeze that resonates to obscure depths I never knew I possessed.

To be loved by you is a privilege.

To love you is consummation.

Our first meeting continues to be one of my fondest memories of her. Of anyone.

Owing to the gift that keeps on giving that is this country's economy, my dad works abroad. Now, amongst the many, many things that hold a marriage together, the occasional carnal indulgence is one of them. Kind of a big one too. So every couple of months, my mom packs her bags, her raunchiest lingerie and best smelling perfume and boards a plane to go see my dad. Yeah, I may also harbour some parental issues. As it happened, she decided to go and have one of these little amatory vacations of hers around the time I came back, leaving me alone at our house to have an erotic rendezvous of my own. The cooperation of our maid cost me ten dollars. Greedy, considering that was a third of her monthly salary but I didn't mind. I'd saved up a decent amount to fund the first few months of my brand-new, state-of-the-art relationship.

I invited Noma over and for our first date, I took her to Imba Matombo. Nice little hotel in the upscale suburbs of Glen Lorne. Cosy place. Overpriced food served in too small portions. Excellent service. Pay a visit. I still remember what we each had. For her, pork ribs, mashed potatoes and a garden salad. I had fries and chicken wings because I always do. And because neither of us had ever had champagne we had that too. A Brut Rosé. We never had champagne again. All in all it cost me seventy-two dollars.

I observed her. Absorbed her. Hell, I practically tattooed her onto my memory. Seeing her for the first time was like finally lifting the veil of distance that had stood between us for all those years. I saw her so clearly: the small chip on her left, foremost incisor, the scar on her forehead that neither she nor her parents knew how she'd got. I soaked in the way her face lit up when she smiled and made me feel like I'd woken up the sunny morning after a rainy night. Click. Save. I keep that image in a special cabinet in my head. It's one of the few things from our time together that I haven't lost or discarded. She was the kind of girl you want all your friends to see you with. This was doubly true for me, the former president of the Nard Committee. You'd be surprised how few guys actually say this about their girlfriends – in their absence – but she was cool. Her personality oozed through her curves and rubbed off on everything around her. I felt renewed, confident. Her laughter continued to ring in your ears long after she'd stopped laughing and it would make you smile just thinking about it. Sometimes, going through the hallways, I hear the echo of her laughter. Shit! Maybe I've come to romanticise what little of her is still in there.

We went back to my place. I'd asked our maid to clean extra thoroughly. She obviously refused so I had to do it myself. I needed some thorough cleaning myself. Shaved a year's worth of pubic and armpit hair and a lifetime's worth of butt hair. Scrubbed myself three times over. Shampooed my hair, trimmed my beard and went and got a haircut. I strategically placed condoms in accessible but discreet places in my room. Set up a couple of scented candles. The only thing missing was roses on the bed.

We didn't have sex that night, but she did enjoy the playlist I'd created for the occasion. I didn't even know what her breasts looked like until three months into our relationship. Still, when it eventually happened … well, that's another thing that's still neatly tucked in my memory files.

Being with her felt surreal. Dreamy. And it was absolutely the wrong kind of foundation for our relationship to be built upon. See, it's a terrible thing to be given something truly amazing. Think of Midas. Think of Icarus. Think of Narcissus. Instead of enjoying her, I ceaselessly waited for the day that I would, in my head, inevitably lose her. I could never shake off the feeling that I was undeserving of her. Never really believed that she could belong to me. Maybe I was right. Or maybe it became a self-fulfilling prophecy. Either way, I was at the finish line before our race even started, just waiting for her to catch up.

Breakups are really unpleasant. Even if you no longer loved the person. I gave her this T-shirt of mine. It had a picture of Harley Quinn on it, and I had another one that had The Joker, and it was supposed to be this cute couples' thing. We only ever wore them at the same time once, but still, it was nice knowing that she had it. It was like acknowledging that she and I were a set, you know? It felt good. It *was* good. After we broke up, I asked for it back. She said no. We haven't spoken since.

There's a Shona proverb; *Ukatsvaka makudo mugomo unomawana* – If you look for baboons in the mountain, you will find them. Ironically this happened while we were on a mountain.

For our birthday, we went hiking. Pasichigare. Imagine an ocean of green upon which slumberous, weathered *dwalas* float wearily that goes on and on until it touches the sky. Close your eyes and listen to the voice of nature. Become lost in the grander scheme of things. Feel infinite. You're at Pasichigare. The idea was hers. It's a testament to just how well she knew me. Obviously when you're at a place like this you'll want to take pictures. Noma always looked good in pictures. And I'm excellent at taking them. I told you, written in the stars.

That little voice that had moved into the pit of my stomach when we started going out decided that was the perfect time to speak up. *Just look at her chats while she's posing for a pic man. Just a peek.* I really don't want to. *Of course that's a fucking lie.* I peeked. Nothing. But I'm not a fucking amateur. Open the archived chats. There is one … uhh … you know what, let's also call this guy Sean. 2. Sean2. His name is next to a smiley emoji with heart eyes. I still hate that emoji even now. I know it's silly but fuck you.

We rented a lodge for the night. Had cake and then sex and then more cake and more sex. Drank ourselves to sleep. I have this weird thing where I always wake up at 3:47 a.m. No matter how late or early I sleep. Even if I was in the middle of a dream. I wake up and I go to the toilet. So that's what I did. I climb back into bed and close my eyes. Guess who? That little voice again. *Her phone's on the charger man. Who's Sean2?*

I'll tell you who Sean2 was. It always bothered me that Noma had so many male friends, but I *had* to be ok with it because dating the best girl in the world and feeling insecure the entire time beats jerking off a number of times a day that is never enough to dampen the constant sense of loneliness that consumes you. I couldn't go back to that. It got to the point where I started talking to my bottle of lube. "Oh, hey there Natasha. How are you this morning? Oh I'm great, I'm just a little thirsty. What's that? You got something that might help?" Yeah, it was bad. Also, pro-tip for my guys out there who do live the life: Use lube. You're welcome.

Sorry for the digression. Sean2. So, she had several guy friends. Occasionally she hung out with them. I tried a few times to do the mature thing and passive-aggressively show her that I wasn't ok with this, but then she would start to get upset. To me, uninitiated as I was to the ways of women and the mechanics of modern day dating, this seemed like a potential threat to some long anticipated respite from my acquaintance with Natasha. So, I had to learn to be ok with it. New Year's Eve, she goes with a group of her friends to some farm that belongs to one of them. They're having a small party. I'm not invited. Fine. I don't like parties anyway. Sean2 is there. They party and drink.

What's a douchebag plus alcohol plus your girlfriend? The answer may surprise you. Ha ha.

She's in tears when she explains to me that she'd had too much to drink but that's not an excuse. Cheaters take note, because this is smart. It lulls me into a false sense of security because

a) She's taking responsibility for her actions and

b) It makes me believe that this was a one-time mistake. She wasn't thinking clearly and as long as I eliminate the parameters that facilitated this chance occurrence, viz. alcohol, Sean2 and a locale that practically instigates one-night stands, then it won't ever happen again.

And I thought I was so much smarter than her. Heh. Additionally, I'm assured that she'd eventually come to her senses before the act could be fulfilled, which translates to: he didn't cum on/in her. Blunder number one. She also swears that it would never have happened again even if I hadn't found out. Blunder number two. While I was going through their message thread, I saw a message where she talked about how long he was able to last in bed. She never said anything like that to me, so thanks Sean2. And there was another one where she was telling him how she was turned on and couldn't wait to see him again. The second is explained away as just a flirtatious message. Sent on a day when she and I had had a fight, one of many. That doesn't make it ok, but it makes it believable. I don't remember how she wiggled out of the first one. In fact, I don't remember much of what we talked about that night. All I know is it's the best sex we ever had.

We continued dating on the condition that she would immediately cut off all communication with Sean2. The few times that I checked her blocked contacts afterwards, I was able to salvage some sense of self-satisfaction when I saw his name there. She was quite convincing the first few weeks following what we thereafter referred to only as 'The Incident'. Calls and dates were more frequent. I had numerous updates of where she was and who she was with. It even got to a point where I felt that *I* was being too dramatic. I almost managed to convince myself that I'd put everything behind us. Almost.

Have you ever watched the sun set? If you just stare at it you won't see the darkness steadily gathering all around you. And then at some point you'll blink and realise, "Oh shit! It's dark out." That's how things happened. I didn't see the sun setting on us until I did. I'm not saying it was her fault entirely. That time that she was making all that effort to convince me that she was sorry, that she still loved me, I enjoyed. I enjoyed it so much, I actually believed that things could continue that way. Where, before, I would have called her every day, wondering where she was, why she wasn't responding to my texts, all the kind of stuff you would expect from your neurotic, decidedly insecure boyfriend, I began expecting her to take on that role. To initiate conversation. To call. To need. To cajole and reassure. I relaxed and stopped trying.

When I finally blinked, the sun was gone. She was suddenly too busy. She had too much work and seldom had time to call me. Her schedule was too tight for her to meet with me. I don't know, maybe I could have saved us. I mentioned before that she made me confident. Confident enough to slide into DMs on Instagram. If she wasn't going to try then neither was I. I was no longer too dependent to see that she was fungible. A lot of the girls I talked to were forgettable and uninteresting. A few were good enough for me to ask for their numbers. One of them gave me. The thrill of talking to her was reminiscent of the times I used to talk to Noma when I first went to China.

The last time I saw her, we went to Imba Matombo to celebrate our one year anniversary. At some point between our unenthusiastic hellos and relieving goodbyes, we each had an epiphany. Hers was that some broken things cannot be fixed. Mine was that they're not worth fixing.

The text came one week later. *I can't do this anymore.* I would be lying if I said that it didn't hurt all the same. Even knowing that, if she hadn't ended things, then I would have.

Love is a lot of things. Real, fake, compromise, sacrifice, forgiveness, dependence, insecurity ... I could go on. It's different for everyone. The only constant is that love is, until it isn't. In the end, all you're left with is a canvass painted by the bright and dull colours of your yesterdays. Even those too will fade... eventually.

It

It fills the emptiness that surrounds me with a void. Its unmoving lips scream whispers into The Silence.

Before I open my eyes, I feel Its presence next to me, familiar; the repugnant familiarity of an enemy one has known for a long time. I inhale. Hold my breath. First, I bring out my right hand. Feel the morning on my skin. Cool. Vast. Celestial. It makes me feel insignificant. Everything stops except my beating heart. I don't get that luxury. I bring out my left and bring the two together in prayer. Search for respite in the darkness behind my eyes. There's nothing there. I misplaced it a long time ago. And then I wrap my fingers around my throat. And squeeze. Feel the walls of my trachea cave under the pressure, close. Tears fill my eyes. My lips start to tingle, going numb. Until my lungs catch fire. I let go.

It watches me, amused.

I open my eyes, simulating the state of being awake, alive. What did I dream about last night? Nothing. I don't dream anymore. It was a dead sleep.

If only it could be permanent.

I turn over to face It. Today it feels more … present, more substantial, more definite.

I reach for my phone and my heart beats a little faster. Time for my daily ritual. Stubbornly, I refuse to acknowledge the small ounce of hope that nudges at me like a child that needs to be attended to. I try, and fail, to stifle it before it can cement itself. Maybe there's a message waiting for me. A good morning. No, that's asking for too much. Too greedy. A reply to a message from yesterday perhaps. That's more realistic. At the very least, a reply to one of the several TikTok videos that I posted on my WhatsApp status. Or my Twitter rant about the new Kanye album. It was trending yesterday. I'll settle for anything. Anything to acknowledge that I exist. There is a WhatsApp icon on my lockscreen notifications. I turn over onto my stomach, poised to text back. I press my thumb onto the glass to unlock the device and the full notification appears. WhatsApp backup in progress. 69% complete.

Of course it is. Who did you think was going to text you?

I ignore It. Ignore, too, the feeling of something of me wasting away; going to sleep. Permanently.

I switch off my mobile data and then on again after a few seconds. The network reception is bad in the area where I live. Maybe some messages didn't arrive. As soon as the symbol for the data connection reappears, my phone vibrates. I close my eyes and silently plead with something that I don't know, something I hope is benevolent.

Just stop doing this to yourself. It's sad.

I read the notification. Message from Reddit. From u/welcomebot: Welcome to r/EbonyAmateurs! In this subreddit we share our love for ebony cuties! Before posting don't forget to read the rules. For more ebony action, check out r/EbonyAmateursGW!

Pathetic. But of course, you would do something like that.

I look at it, irate, into Its hollow eyes. It reaches out and then in, holding something, and places it into my heart. I know what it is. I recognise the sharp edges. I've been cut by them before. Defeat. I put it aside, where I can easily get it again when the time comes.

I click on the notification, which takes me to r/EbonyAmateurs. The first post is a picture, the thumbnail showing a girl lying on a bed, her legs spread and bent so far up that her feet are almost touching her ears. The title reads: Be honest, would you fuck or taste it first? [F19] I scroll through the subreddit mechanically, ignoring the numerous pictures, videos and GIFs of naked girls contorted in various 'sexy' positions, some that I find impressive and others that are almost comical. After a while, I change the post sorting to show the all-time top posts. I see more of the same content until I come to a picture of a girl standing in what looks like a basketball court, wearing black leggings and a neon green crop top, the index and middle finger of her raised left hand extended in a peace sign. She is smiling, revealing a set of perfect teeth. The smile reminds me of Fiona. She always had the most beautiful smile. The girl's username is Chocolate_Nymph. The post title reads austerely: Cute ebony babe. I download the picture before I zoom onto her face. She looks young, younger than nineteen. I scroll down. Her ass is turned towards the camera. It's not particularly big, even with the way she is slightly bent forward to accentuate it. Through the thin fabric of the leggings, I can see the faint outline of her underwear.

I feel a stir, like a small creature rousing from sleep. I continue staring at her, undressing her, imagining the colour of her underwear, whether they are lace or cotton, until I feel myself fully engorged, the thump-thumping of my heart in sync with the throbbing between my legs. I switch my phone to my left hand and use my right to pull down my boxer shorts. I take one last look at her, absorb her, before I close my eyes and begin to fondle myself…

Two minutes later, I'm panting like a thirsty dog, struggling to catch my breath. I try not to measure the amount of time. Try to convince myself that it'd be different if it was the real thing. I don't believe myself. I feel a tension lift off my shoulders, and for those priceless few seconds, a lightness washes over me, spreading outwards from my now limp penis and through my body like a ripple. I want to grab it, trap it inside me before it all goes away, like dew in the morning, but it's so light it slips through my desperate reach.

I look at the thick, white pool of shame that has collected on my navel and other drops of it that are all over my torso, as far up as my chest.

You are disgusting.

I look around for something nearby to clean myself with. There is nothing. Careful not to let any of it dribble onto the bed, I kick off my boxers, slide off the bed and walk quickly towards my wardrobe where I keep a roll of toilet paper. I wipe myself and crunch the toilet paper into a ball before I throw it into the trash can that I keep in my room. It's filled with other balls of toilet paper that are starting to turn yellow and let off a stale, salty stench that makes me gag.

You are rotten.

I catch a glimpse of myself in the full-length mirror on the door of my wardrobe. I pause to study myself. At five feet nine, I could hardly be considered short. My shoulders are broad, my stomach flat. I flex it, and run my fingers over the set of six clearly defined abs that appears. Even though I'm not particularly muscular, my body is lean and athletic. Fiona used to call it a swimmer's body. I can't swim. She said it's the kind of body that could be on the cover of a men's health magazine. The headline: Get your summer body in only 30 days with this workout plan. Even some guys had commented on my physique when I still went to the gym. Said they wanted to have a body like mine. "Not those jacked steroid bodies," one guy had said.

Yet nobody wants you. All this effort to look attractive.

Maybe if I had a beard. Girls like men with beards. They're all the rage these days. My face is smooth as an egg. I look a lot younger than my twenty-six years. Like Ansel Elgort. Or Asa Butterfield. I wonder if they wish they had beards.

I see It in the mirror, standing behind me, looming, draining all the colour and light from the room. I look away. But I feel It, tracing a piercing appendage over my body, leaving invisible cuts that I feel under my skin. It lingers longer on my vanity places, the ones where I try to salvage some self-esteem: my biceps, my shoulders, my abs, everything that should, in theory and according to prevailing trends, make me attractive. It goes further down, stops and smiles.

You seem a little lacking here, a little inadequate.

I sigh and walk away from the mirror. I pick out some clothes and get dressed. I check my phone again. No new notifications.

Duh.

I sit down at my desk and open my laptop. The notification tray is bombarded by a mix of emails from education websites advertising universities that are currently open for application submissions, some with scholarship offers and others from job websites notifying me about vacancies. I dismiss them.

All you do is sit on your ass.

There is a notification from my torrent downloading application that my download for the final season of The Leftovers is complete and is now seeding. I open the application and stop the seeding process. I open the folder to make sure all the episodes have been fully downloaded before I can start today's scheduled task of sending out university applications. I can feel It lingering behind me, feel Its glare on the nape of my neck, probing me.

I go back to my emails and click on one of the links, which takes me to the website of a university in Ireland. I browse through the requirements for my program. I meet all of them: a minimum of a second class bachelor's degree, a certification of English proficiency, academic transcript, CV bla bla bla. I read through the application process quickly and check that there is a scholarship option before I open the application portal and start filling in my details. First are the personal details.

Well this is ambitious.

Then contact details.

Haven't you already done this?

Educational background and qualifications.

You know how this ends.

Work Experience (optional).

There we go.

I stare at the blinking cursor until my eyes start to water. I could already see the response, like many others that I had already got: We are pleased to inform you that you have been accepted at our university. However, you do not have enough qualifications to be eligible for a scholarship and you will need to pay the full tuition amount of $XXX.

I feel tired, like the full burden of the future I have imagined in my head is a physical thing that has been placed on my shoulders. I'm too exhausted to continue doing anything else. I decide to take a break and watch one episode of The Leftovers.

When our maid knocks on my door to announce that tea is ready, I'm halfway through the third episode.

You're a fucking disappointment. Lazy piece of shit.

In our house, meals are eaten in silence.

For some reason, no one ever thinks to turn on the radio or TV when we eat. We listen to the sound of each other's chewing and swallowing and gulping down water, the occasional scraping of a plate or the clink of metal against china. It makes me think of the digestion process that we learned about in high school biology. The section diagram of a person cut right along the length of the oesophagus; a lump of food shown in different stages of digestion.

It's the kind of silence that settles on the room when you walk in while people are talking about you. Or when you've done something wrong and you know you have been caught and it's only a matter of time before the matter is brought up. A pregnant silence. Holding us hostage in its cavernous spaces. Covering everything in a nice, even, thick layer of tension.

It interprets my parents' silence for me, sitting in between the three of us, vast and insurmountable.

You're overstaying your welcome.

I look at Father. He's not here. He rarely ever is. He's only present when he starts talking about something that he's passionate about. Usually politics. Sometimes his parents. He must be thinking about work, or the state of the economy, or what he calls 'The Black Problem.' He thinks about the world and the future and the grander scheme. He travels a lot, physically and mentally. For him, there's always more to be done. And failing to do so has consequences. When I was a child, those consequences were a metre long and made of leather.

Mother refuses to meet my eyes.

Sometimes, I think that she sees It too. The few times that her eyes meet mine. The most terrifying thing at those times is that she seems to *know* It. It seems, for a brief moment, as if she wants to tell me something. But before I can decide if it really is recognition I detect on her face, she always shakes her head and looks away again.

Sometimes I have trouble remembering her voice.

She doesn't look at me as she speaks. "Son, how are the university applications going?"

Father raises his head slightly. He comes just a little bit closer.

"Ok." I don't elaborate further. She doesn't ask me to.

Father turns to me. It's as if he is seeing me after a very long time. "What about jobs?"

"Nothing yet." He lingers just for a while before he goes away again.

They don't want you here anymore. You're a parasite.

Mother takes a sip of her tea. I look up, in time to see her turning her head away. In the instant before she does, I see that look again in her eyes, sort of like we're compatriots meeting in a foreign land. The one that says, I too have seen what you have seen, I understand. And I know. She has It too. She must. We continue the meal in silence, each of us relieved and glad for the return to normalcy. I barely touch my food. Mother too. When I go back to my room, I try to remember what her voice had sounded like. All I hear is a distorted echo.

My room is a mess.

Just like you.

I don't remember the last time I made the bed. The laundry that the maid washed and ironed for me a week ago is still on the sofa, already starting to wrinkle. I haven't swept the floor for over a week and a fine layer of dust coats the floor, broken occasionally by several of my footprints. With the curtains still drawn, the lighting of the room reminds me of the way that my dreams look. The smell from the trash can is suddenly unbearable.

I tell myself that I will clean up. Tomorrow. Today I don't have the energy. I feel like a flower that has not been watered for too long. I just want to lie down. It takes my hand and leads me to the bed. I let myself fall onto it and I land on my face. My feet remain dangling over the edge of the bed. I can't be bothered to lift them up.

A silence follows.

God, you're pathetic. Look at yourself. You're almost thirty and you have nothing to show for all the time that you've spent taking up space in the world. When you die, which cannot happen quickly enough, people will come to your funeral and they're going to wonder, 'Who was he?' and anyone who's seen you will say, 'He was here. He was with us the whole time.' They aren't going to be convinced, those that will have asked, and they will want to know still, 'But who WAS he?' and nobody will really know or have the honesty to say you were nobody. No one will say you were attractive because that is not what is going to matter. You can work out all you want. No one will remember how you had a nice set of abs. You're like those big round oranges that are bigger and more orange than all the others, but when you take a bite, they have no taste. They taste like water. You have no substance. You have no one. You have nothing better to do except feel sorry for yourself and make up excuses for why your life is so shitty. Rotten. Boring. Miserable.

I grab a pillow and press it to my face. I scream until my throat hurts.

The Letter

The fierce October afternoon sun gently parts the old woman's eyes, the harshness of it subdued and tinted a soft, murky yellow by her bedroom curtains, and pulls her tentatively from the dream she had been having. She cannot remember the dream, but she can see that she had slept fitfully. The fabric of her dress is plastered against the skin of her back, like the hair on a wet dog, even though she had only used a thin linen sheet to cover her legs, which was now in a crumpled pile on the floor. The fan whirs lightly from its position on the floor, to the right of her bed, sending an occasional draught of cool air in her direction briefly before the torpid summer heat settles over her again, as the fan continues its sweeping motion. It is the same fan she had insisted to Zviko she did not need, but had come to appreciate each day that the year's heat wave had gone on. The heaviness of sleep still lingers in the room, feeling like sand in her eyes and making her feel as if she is under water. She rolls onto her back to stretch her arms and winces when she feels something dig into the left side of her torso. She reaches for the object and her hand lands on the faux leather cover of her King James bible. She pulls it from underneath her, frowning when she notices that the front cover and a few pages have been crushed into a fold on one corner.

From the street outside, the excited chatter of children coming back from school clambers over the Durawall and reaches her bedroom at the back of the house. The noise scatters the haunting sense that the things from her forgotten dream were still in the room with her, stalking her from her peripheral, slowly edging towards her. She closes her eyes and listens to the children, lets their chatter find its way to her and sifts through it, separating it into individual voices, untangling the single mass of sound and laughter into distinct words, stories, beings. She continues to hear them even after the children and their voices have faded into the distance.

The children meant it was a short while past two o'clock now. She had not intended to sleep for so long. She had not intended to sleep at all. One moment she had been reading her bible, preparing for the next day's cell group meeting, and the next she was waking up. Tafadzwa would be home any minute. Yawning, she swings her legs over the edge of the bed. She stands up and looks around for her slippers.

Still not yet fully awake, she is momentarily stunned when a sound suddenly erupts through the stillness of the room. It takes her a moment, as it always does, to register that it is her cell phone's ringtone, a song by someone called Zahara that Tafadzwa set for whenever Zviko was calling, so that she would know who it was without needing to squint at the screen. Her granddaughter was thoughtful like that; always trying to make her life easier, something she needed at her age and in her condition. The old woman was not particularly old, younger even, than a lot of the other grandmothers she knew from her church. But none of those other women had had their heads cut open. She was only sixty-seven, but already her eyesight, her memory, her entire body, was failing. She could not now see herself living to be the energetic, spirited old woman she had always thought she would become, as her own grandmother, Mbuya Garikai, had been. A result of the sedentary life she had been forced to live, firstly on the advice of her doctor and then the insistence of Zviko, until eventually her body would not allow her to have any say in the matter. She had watched, first with denial, then alarm and finally prostration as her once lean figure softened, widened and drooped, as layers of flabby, soft flesh grew on her arms and thighs and stomach.

She hobbles to the dressing table next to her bed and picks up her phone. Holding it carefully in her tremulous left hand, she raises it towards her face and then taps the red button with the index finger of her right. She shouts hello several times into the blackness of the cold glass rectangle pressed against her cheek before she remembers that the green button is the one that she is supposed to press to answer calls. Having forgotten how to make a call and without Tafadzwa to assist her, she has to wait for Zviko to call again.

The blue heel of one of her slippers is protruding from underneath the foot of the bed. Slowly, she bends one knee, groaning, her knee feeling like a rusty door hinge. She is in this position, already panting, drops of sweat starting to dot her, when her phone rings again. She curses silently and begins to straighten up. A sudden sharp pain flashes along her spine and she lets out a sound, "like the bellowing of a dying cow," Tafadzwa would later tell her mother, and falls forward, landing on her elbows.

The door to her bedroom swings open. The old woman can make out the silhouette of her granddaughter standing in the doorway, her satchel dangling from her left hand. She notes how Tafadzwa's maroon skirt now stops above the knees and the part of her white shirt above her breasts is stretched, the button on the verge of falling off. She would need to tell Zviko to buy a new uniform.

Tafadzwa drops the satchel and rushes to her aid. "Gogozani, why are you on the floor?"

"I fell down. I was trying to get my slippers from under the bed and I fell down. Old age is eating me."

"Don't you always say that you are still a young girl." Tafadzwa giggles impishly.

"That is true. It is my wish, but my body does not agree with me anymore. Now help me up."

Tafadzwa kneels down and extends her arm. The old woman sits up cautiously, feeling her joints, and grabs her granddaughter's arm. She places another hand on the bed and struggles to get her legs underneath her. A fetid smell fills the room. Tafadzwa pretends not to notice it. The old woman feels the sting of tears in her eyes. Eventually, she manages to stand up. "Thank you, my child. Thank you *Soko*."

"You do not need to thank me Gogozani."

"No, it is witchcraft to not give thanks when it is due. How was school today?"

"It was ok. Are you ok? Do you feel pain anywhere?"

The old woman laughs, a clucking sound that quickly turns into bursts of violent dry coughs that makes the contents of her head clutter against her skull. When she recovers after a few moments, Tafadzwa is standing next to her with a glass of water. She smiles as she takes the glass from her and places it on her lap, holding it with both hands, but not drinking it. She feels her granddaughter's eyes on her, the same questions she had already asked being reflected in her eyes – big eyes, like Zviko's which she herself had got from her father – which are shimmering with worry.

"Do not worry my child. I am ok. You know these old bones, they have felt the heat of the sun for too long."

"Should I call Mhamha?"

"No." The old woman cannot help feeling that her response was too unnecessarily loud. "You do not need to worry her. I am sure she has a lot to do at work. We should keep this between us *handiti ka?*"

Tafadzwa looks at the floor. "Where are the slippers you were trying to get?"

"Right there. Just reach under the bed, you will find them." As the old woman watches her granddaughter effortlessly retrieve the slippers, she feels the pang of having lost something to the past. Tafadzwa places the slippers at her feet.

"Have you eaten yet my child? I was going to cook but I fell asleep. I will prepare something for you now." The old woman starts to stand up. Her bowels loosen again.

"Gogozani, you know you are not supposed to cook."

"I know, but I am your grandmother. I should be cooking for you. You need to put some flesh on those bones if the boys are going to look at you. You are already a young woman *haikona*. I will be expecting a son in law to come knocking on my door soon."

Tafadzwa's subtle smile is diffident. "Mhamha will not like it if she hears that you are working. You should rest. I will make something for you."

"*Ewoo.* Do you people want to kill me? Is this living? I will become a cripple from sitting for so long."

Tafadzwa ignores her. "There is some *mutakura* in the fridge. I will heat it up for you." Before she can respond, her granddaughter glides out of the room.

She looks around, wondering what it was she had been doing before. As if to answer her, her phone starts ringing once more. She shuffles slowly to the dressing table and picks it up. She is careful to press the green button.

As was almost customary, by the time the phone reaches the old woman's ear, her daughter is already partway through a sentence. "…wrong? I have been calling you. Are you ok?"

"He … hello. Hellooo! Can you hear me? Zviko, are you hearing me?"

"Yes, Mhai, I can hear you clearly. You do not need to shout." Regardless of how many times Tafadzwa tried to explain it to her, the old woman could not understand how she could talk to someone far away as if they were right next to her. "Why did you not answer your phone?"

"I was sleeping … on the couch. You know my ears are not what they used to be. I used to have the ears of a rabbit but now I am almost deaf. How are you Zviko."

"I am well. How is Tafa?"

"She is well. She has just come from school."

"At this time? She is supposed to come straight home after her last class. She cannot traipse around with her friends when she knows you are home alone."

"Oh just let her be Zviko. You yourself did not listen to me either. She is a good girl. Besides, a child deserves to have a childhood."

"She needs to be taking care of you, Mhai."

"I can take care of myself." The old woman thinks of herself on the floor only a few moments ago.

There is a brief pause on the other end of the line. Her daughter is quite intuitive when it comes to her or perhaps it is simply the result of her having been around her for so long. She can always see through her lies.

"Mhai, I want to talk to you about something."

"Ohh. What is it? Is everything alright?"

"Everything is fine Mhai. I am coming after work. I will tell you in person."

"Zviko, you sound troubled. And you know that makes me troubled."

She hears her daughter sigh, blowing the static of the unstable network connection into her ear. "That is precisely why it is better if I tell you in person Mhai."

"Stop treating me like a child Zvikomborero!"

She had not meant to shout. It was something she had started doing after the surgery. She was wont to sudden burst of emotions that she could not control and it felt as if an invader was residing in her body, pressing buttons that made her heart, mind and body do things that she did not want them to. But she was too stubborn to apologise or explain herself. She could not live with people knowing that her mind was going.

There is a long pause as her daughter deliberates over what to do. "Ok. I will tell you but I will ask Mai Tino to come over and look after you until I arrive."

"There is no need for that Zvikomborero. I do not need anyone else to look after me. I have Tafadzwa."

A quiet settles once more on their conversation, like a sea of static that stands deep and wide between two lovers. "I received a letter."

The old woman hears the darkness in her daughter's voice and shudders. "From who?"

"Baba."

As if the door had suddenly been shut on a rainy day, all the aching in the old woman's body quiets down and is replaced by a denseness in her chest that feels like a solid shadow. Her mouth becomes dry and she stumbles backward, suddenly feeling as if the world is alive and moving underneath her, as if she is standing on water.

She sits on the bed. "Is he … Did he … Where is … When did you receive it?"

"A few days ago."

"And you only thought to tell me this now?"

"Mhai, I had to work. I wanted to wait until the weekend so I could come and be with you."

"I am sorry. I am just…" Was she surprised? Relieved? She had known, or felt rather, that he was still out there in the world. There had been rumours too. Some people claimed to have seen him. But what she had felt was stronger than that. It was like knowing the touch of your lover even when your eyes were closed. She was not angry either. Even when he had … even then, she had not had the strength to conjure such an emotion. It had simply left her weakened and drained. What she felt was something plucked from the dusky space between reminiscence and loss.

"What did the letter say?"

"I don't know. I didn't read it."

"You haven't?"

"Yes. And I'm not even sure that I want to. There is nothing that he can say that will make up for what he did."

The old woman wonders if she too might be better off not knowing. She had almost healed; almost forgotten. No good ever came of opening up old wounds. Yet she needed to know. She needed to understand. She had been so certain of his love for her. His devotion to them. He had never given her any reason to doubt him and she never had. Yet… there was this letter. Coming to remind her that perhaps she should have. That something she had not known all along must have been very wrong otherwise there would have been no need for this letter at all. She needed to know what that thing was. She needed to finally be able to close the door to the past that she had held open for so long.

She wanted to know what her husband had to say for himself. Whether he would ask for her forgiveness. Or if he would want to come back. Would she be able to accept him? Was she ready to forgive him? Would she even need to?

"Mhai. Mhai are you still there?"

"Yes, Zvikomborero. I am here. I am just… thinking. This is not a small thing that you have just told me."

"This is why I wanted to tell you in person. I knew you would start to think about useless things. Someone needs to be there to look after you."

"You do not need to worry about me, Zviko. I have Tafadzwa. It is you I should be worrying about."

"Me?"

"He left us both."

"Oh. I am fine." The old woman senses that a light has dimmed in her daughter.

"Anyway, what time are you coming? Let me prepare something for you to eat. Sadza and mushrooms? You always liked that." Her daughter's response only reaches her as an unintelligible buzz, the phone already on the bed, followed soon after, by her own body which makes the bed creak as she lands.

She remains that way for a while, staring up at the ceiling, at the endless white sea that seems to be alive, falling towards her, threatening to crush her and then rising again. Slowly, she rises and wipes her eyes with the back of her hand. She walks to the bathroom and bangs the door shut behind her.

Hesitantly, the old woman faces the bathroom mirror. A woman peers back at her, a stranger. The stranger shares most of the same features as herself, from what she can remember of her face. Like the pea sized mole between her left eye and her nose. She has her light skin, peppered with black spots, but there are wrinkles at the corners of the woman's eyes and mouth. Her face is also small, oval shaped, disproportionate to her plump figure. Her short hair is not combed or covered by a doek. The stranger has a scar on her right temple, a C-shaped incision and her skull is depressed under it, as if someone had hit her head with a small, rounded object and the skull had collapsed. The black pools of the woman's are distant, and seem to be looking at her from far away. They seem lost, detached, focused less on what they saw, and more on keeping whatever lay in those two black pools at bay.

She turns the knob of the sink. It sputters, coughs and lets out a few drops of water before it sighs wearily and gives up. She remembers that it is Friday, one of the five days of the week that they do not have water. It only comes on Sundays and Wednesdays. She looks about and finds the bucket of water next to the toilet bowl that was meant to be used to flush the toilet. She bends forward, closes her eyes and splashes some water onto her face. It feels refreshing against her burning skin. Without opening them, she stands up and extends her hand outward until it touches the rough surface of the untiled bathroom wall. With her eyes closed, she feels her way out of the bathroom.

She totters into the living room where Tafadzwa is sitting on the floor next to her shaky coffee table, one of whose legs has been replaced by a half brick. A pile of textbooks and an open exercise book is spread in front of her. She is punching numbers into her calculator. She looks up when the old woman walks in.

"The food is almost ready. It will just be a few more minutes."

"Oh, you do not need to trouble yourself my child. I am not hungry. It is you who needs to eat."

"Gogozani, you have to eat. You know what the doctor said."

"These doctors of yours don't know anything. They said I should rest and now it is killing me. A person should only rest when their creator calls them to rest and not before. What I need is some hard day's work. As long as one works, their flesh will heal itself."

Tafadzwa stands up. "If you want we can take a walk, but only after you have eaten."

"You and your mother are the same. You are stubborn."

"And where do you think we got it from?"

The old woman smiles. Immediately her face darkens. "Your mother called me just now. She said she is coming."

"Is that who you were talking to? What time is she coming?"

"She did not say. But I want you to go to the shops and buy some mushrooms. You know she likes those. Go into my bedroom and get my purse from … from…" The old woman looks about her.

"You do not have a purse Gogozani." Tafadzwa speaks to the ground at her feet.

"No. No. I do. Every time I come back from work, I put it…"

"Have you taken your pills?"

"No. My purse is just…" She looks at her hands. Tafadzwa's voice reaches her as if from behind a closed door.

"I know where it is. I will get it for you. You just sit down."

"There is five dollars in there."

Tafadzwa disappears for a few moments and reappears, holding a small transparent box in one hand and a ten dollar note in the other. "There was no five dollars, but there was this ten."

"Okay. But make sure they give you the change for it. Sometimes they try to steal from me because they think I am a forgetful old woman. But I am sharp."

"Yes, Gogozani. And you should take these after you have eaten, okay?" Tafadzwa hands her the transparent plastic box. Its contents rattle as her trembling hand takes it and places it next to her on the sofa.

Tafadzwa disappears again. She returns with a plate piled with the steaming mix of *nyimo, magwere, nyemba* and *nzungu* and a cup of water that she places on the stool and sets in front of her.

"Will you not turn on the TV?" The silence was beginning to trouble the old woman.

"There is no electricity. I think it is a fault somewhere. This is now the second day."

"You can turn on the solar. Baa Zviko wanted to buy a generator but I told him that solar is better. It costs more to put it up but you do not need to keep buying fuel for it."

Tafadzwa looks up from her homework which she was still doing even as she ate. She feigns a weak, specious smile. "We do not have that anymore Gogozani."

"What? Was it stolen? But these children of nowadays *ka*, you would think they do not have mothers."

"We do not live in that house anymore. Don't you remember?"

"Oh?"

"We moved. After..." Tafadzwa pushes the food around her plate with her fork.

"Ohh. Now I remember. I remember."

The old woman, feeling the onset of a headache coming, presses an index and middle finger against her temple. Absentmindedly, she gently rubs the raised tissue of the scar where the doctors had sewn her up, circling the groove where part of her had been cut away, a part which now seemed to have contained some essence of her very being. She felt she was no longer complete.

Before her surgery, she had been a history and literature teacher at Oriel Girls High School. She had not worried too much when she started getting the headaches. She thought that it was perhaps because of work related stress. "I am just getting old," she had told Baa Zviko when he had urged her to go and see a doctor. She had never been one to rush to a hospital or take medication for her illnesses unless it became absolutely necessary. Then one day, during one of her classes, she fainted.

She had been diagnosed with a ruptured brain aneurysm, one that needed immediate surgery. Their entire savings could barely cover half the cost of the operation. They had sold their car and their small stand in Damafalls at a reduced price because they needed the money urgently. Even then, they had still needed to borrow some more from relatives and friends. But what it had eventually cost her was far worse than financial. Maybe it would have been better if she had died.

"What did you say?" The old woman whips her head sideways and finds her granddaughter staring at her, her eyes wide open. She had not realised she had spoken out loud.

"Oh. I am just thinking, my child."

"About what?"

"Your grandfather."

"Do you miss him?"

"I don't know."

"It is not good for you to think about him. And to think about things that happened long ago."

"But it happened, my child. It happened. And we cannot hide from it."

"We can leave it as it is."

"Mmmm."

"You should not feel responsible for him leaving. It was not your fault."

The old woman looks at her granddaughter and shakes her head tiredly. Following the logic of cause and effect, a straight line could be drawn between everything that had happened and her illness. If she had not got sick, her husband would not have left. If she had listened to him and gone to see the doctor when he said, she might not have ended up needing the operation.

"No one knows whose fault it was. Only God knows what happened."

"You should take your pills."

Tafadzwa stands up and collects their empty plates. The old woman opens the box of pills and slowly, tracing a finger over each word, reads the days marked on the top of each small compartment. Friday's morning pills are still there.

"Let me help you." Tafadzwa kneels in front of her and takes the pills from the box one by one, placing them in her open palm. There are four in total.

"Thank you." The old woman carefully places the pills in her mouth and then takes the water. She spills a few drops onto her lap as she drinks it. She hands the cup back to Tafadzwa. After a short while, she begins to feel drowsy.

"Mhai." Someone is nudging her shoulder gently. She blinks her eyes at Zviko's face peering at her. The room is dark. "Mhai, wake up. It's me."

"When did you arrive? I was talking to Tafadzwa just now. Where has she gone?"

"She is in the kitchen, cooking." The old woman can hear the sound of the gas stove hissing and her granddaughter humming a familiar tune.

"How are you? Did you travel well?"

"I am well. If your day has been well?"

"My day was well."

Zviko rises and walks into the darkness. She reappears with a lamp that she places on the coffee table. "Don't you see this is better now?"

"So, where is it?"

"Mhai don't you think it is best if we wait until the electricity comes back. You will not see anything with this light."

"There hasn't been electricity for two days now."

"Then wait until the morning."

"I cannot. I will not sleep tonight. I need to know."

Zviko sighs and the old woman knows she will have her way. She watches her daughter stand up to bring the lamp closer, her mind racing, conjuring reasons and explanations for her husband's sudden departure, imagining the contents of the letter.

He had just left, like a limb being severed, he was there and then he was not. There was no ceremony, no farewell, no warning. He did not take anything with him, not even his wallet. She simply woke up one morning and he was just not there. He left a bank statement showing the sale of their house and the purchase of the smaller one that she now lived in. That was the only evidence they had that he had not been killed or taken against his will; he had known what he was doing. At the time, she had not yet fully recovered her memory following the surgery and the significance of his disappearance had been lost on her. When Zviko explained to her what had happened it had been as if she was telling her a story that had happened in a book, to a fictional character whose problems were only as real as the imagination of the author made them. When she did eventually comprehend it, the shock and gravity of it had been blunted by her being accustomed to his absence. She could only remember him in a blurred way, like remembering a dream.

Zviko holds the lamp with one hand and extracts a brown envelope from her purse. It is still sealed. She turns it over in her hand.

The old woman asks, "Is there an address?"

"Tafadzwa found it at the door."

"Tafa– You mean it was delivered here? He was here? Do not tell me." The old woman's chest becomes too small for what is inside it.

"I told her to give it to me when she called to tell me about it."

"Did she read it?"

"She says she did not."

Zviko traces a hand over the lettering on the front, her father's name. The lap's light looks like a lost moon trapped in her eyes. Abruptly, she tears it open, breathing heavily. She places it in the old woman's outstretched palm.

Slowly, her hands trembling, she unfolds the two pages. There is nothing familiar about the handwriting. She gestures for Zviko to bring the light closer.

She begins to read the letter, mouthing the words quietly, her eyes gleaming in the lamp's light.

Burnt Pot

You watch, a wide-eyed disjointed observer, as your life forms a pool around your legs. The halo of tragedy indenting a poignant finale. You see, somewhere in the haze, your mother's face looking down at you, grave and disapproving, and you want to apologise for everything. But your lips are too weak to form the words; your tongue feels like a rock inside your mouth. With damned certainty you know that all you will ever feel is this sensation of a fire ravaging you from the inside.

Looking back, the day your world erupted in flames is the day you let a pot of chicken stew burn in your sister's house. But in truth, the spark was ignited the night you sat in a dim, smoky hut with your mother, cloaked in the shadow of a future that had abruptly taken an unwelcome turn.

On the day that you burnt the pot of chicken stew, you raced to the kitchen only to find black lumps the colour of charcoal glued to a layer of soot on the floor of the pot.

As if on cue, the arrival of your sister was announced by Mai Gamu, the woman who lives in the flat directly below yours, on the ground floor of the apartment building in which you and your sister live.

"Ehh. How was your day Madam?" Everybody in the apartment, except you, calls your sister madam because she is a Geography and History teacher at Glen View High 1. That and the fact that she has no husband. When you think of a madam you imagine a bespectacled, sophisticated woman, trim, tall, embellished by a grace that veils a subdued but perceptible severity. Your sister is nothing like that. A short, rotund woman, almost twice your width but a finger shorter, whose dark skin only barely contains the contents of her rudimentary character. She is hurriedly efficient, lacking any kind of consideration for aesthetics or what image she projects to onlookers. As far as she is concerned, they ought to mind their own business.

"Mmm *amai.* It was so so. At this point it is enough just to be breathing."

"Why do you say that Madam? Are things not well at school?"

"Is it only at school that they are not well? Are we not living in the same country Mai Gamu?"

"Ahh *nhai* Madam. Are you going to start weeping for this country today? For some of us the tears have already dried up. But tell me, what happened?" Mai Gamu's notoriety for wresting private details about people's lives that she could later divulge at a hairdresser's or to her fellow Daughters of Ebenezer during their Friday cell group meetings was well known around the neighbourhood. This had the effect of making her simultaneously popular and unpopular depending on whether or not you were the recipient or the subject of her gossiping. One who did not know her better could easily mistake her intrusiveness for genuine concern.

A few days after you arrived, you met her while you were coming back from watering the tomatoes in your sister's garden. She invited you in to have a cup of juice. "Come in my child. You look tired and it is very hot today." You were slightly uncertain, not because you had any qualms about accepting food from a stranger, but because you were unsure how your sister would feel about it.

She noticed your hesitation. "Don't worry. Madam and I are like belt and trousers. She is my *sahwira*. We are *bests of*. Besides, she has gone out, hasn't she?"

You thought for a moment, "Yes, she has. She went to town."

She smiled as she gestured for you to enter, the sort of smile one would have after reacquainting with a close friend that has been gone for a long time. The dual dining and living room had the smell of old newspapers and beans from the silver pot that you spotted on the stove as you walked in. Even with the windows wide open, the heat of the early January sun pervaded the room with malignant intensity. "So, what is your name my child?" she called out from the kitchen.

"My name is Rudo."

"*Inga* you have a nice name Rudo. I am Mai Gamu."

"Pleased to meet you, Mai Gamu," you reply, clapping your hands quietly although she could neither see nor hear you.

"Yes, we neighbours should get to know each other. You never know when you need something. It will not be proper if you start introducing yourself the day that you need to borrow some sugar. Is that not so?"

"Yes." She came out of the kitchen and handed you a perspiring glass of Mazoe orange crush. You stood up and curtsied as you received it.

"*Inga* you have good manners. Most children these days do not even bother to say thank you." You sit back down, not sure what response she expects from you. You are adept at only saying the things that you know adults want to hear. Your mother taught you that.

Before the silence could stretch to awkwardness, she asked, "So what is your relationship with my *sahwira* Rudo? Is she your aunt? Your sister? Or maybe she is your mother, you never know." She chuckled and inexplicably, you thought of a hyena.

"I am her sister."

"Hoo *nhai*. How come I have never heard of you or seen you before? I know her other sister who comes here sometimes. Patience? Prudence?"

"It's Prisca. We do not have the same mother."

"Okay, okay," she said, nodding slowly. "I see. How did that happen? Does your father have many wives or there was some mischief involved?" She smiled again, a mischievous twinkle dancing in her eyes and the image of a hyena returned.

It was the same image you had thought of when your mother had told you the story of the hyena and the cow. The hyena was invited to a feast by her friends. It was to a very faraway place and the hyena had recently given birth to a hyena cub. She could not travel the long journey with her cub so she went to her friend, the cow and asked her to watch her cub until she returned. The cow agreed. The hyena went to her feast and did not come back for three weeks even though she had promised the cow that it would only take three days. After some time passed, the cow too gave birth to a calf. Soon afterwards, the cow was invited to a wedding. Because the wedding was in a faraway land, the cow could not take her calf with her so she went to her friend, the hyena and asked her to look after her calf while she was gone. The hyena agreed. The cow went to the wedding, but when she returned, the hyena had eaten her calf and run away to live in the jungle. And that is why the hyena and the cow do not see each other to this day.

You thought of the hyena, smiling its hyena smile as it agreed to look after the cow's calf.

You drank the rest of the juice in one gulp and clapped your hands quickly before you thanked her and announced that you needed to get going.

"Already? When did we get to know each other *ipapa*?"

"I need to start preparing supper."

"Hoo alright. I see my *sahwira* has already started putting you to work. She is very strict that one and she can be a little scary. You should come back some time. And if there is anything you need my child, just come to me *handiti ka*."

"Yes ma'am."

After that day, she became a familiar and friendly face. Someone to talk to. But you kept the details of your relationship with her from your sister. You were sure she would see your visits to the woman's house as time wasting. She often complained that you were lazy and spent too much time sitting in front of the TV instead of working or reading your books.

Your sister sucked air through her teeth, lamenting the current state of affairs of not only her life but the country that she held responsible for her ill fortune, but she did not answer Mai Gamu's question. "*Amai ka*. Mmm. My blood pressure will increase if I even talk about this. Let me keep my words. Anyway, let me go and see what this child has done now. I can see some smoke coming out from the kitchen window. *Ende zvakaoma*."

As your sister slowly hobbled up the stairs, groaning as her arthritic legs laboured to support her weight, you thought about how you ended up in this place that had, since your arrival, always felt on the verge of caving underneath your feet.

Sisi Memo was hardly your sister, least of all because you did not have the same mother. She was well in her forties by the time you were born, already married and widowed and what little interaction you had with her prior to living with her had been during her yearly Christmas visits. Even then, it was limited to mostly formal greetings and courteous goodbyes. So you were taken by surprise when, the Christmas after you had finished your form two, your mother told you that she would be taking you to live with her in the city.

"Why Mhamha? I don't even know her."

"What does that matter? She is your father's child and she has already agreed to take you with her."

"Why should I be taken? What is wrong with me staying here? No Mhamha, I don't want to go."

Your mother had looked at you in the way that she often did that suggested that she had something to say to you, but that you were too young to be able to understand. She had sighed and stared at you, a solemn look that seemed to be searching for something inside of you that was not yet there, something that if only you were to have, you would appreciate the words that she now could not say to you.

"It is not about what you want *mwanangu*. It is about what is best for you. You are my eldest child. You will need to take care of your brothers and sisters just like Memo has done. And you are about to start your form three. You need to go to a better school. Plus, your sister is a teacher. She can help you with your books better than I can."

"Baba can help me. He got to standard seven, didn't he?"

Your mother had laughed, a dry cackle that culminated in a series of violent coughs. "Where do you think he will find time between farm work and taking care of your siblings? Listen to me, my daughter. Do you think I would do anything that was not with your best interests at heart? Eh?"

"What if she kills me? The way that she..." Your mother had shot you a glare that caused your tongue to shrivel in your mouth.

It was true that your sister's husband had died before his time, but his struggle with diabetes had been a matter of public record. Yet this did nothing to silence the whispers about how your sister had taken him because she wanted the plot of land that he had left for her in his will. She had conveniently done so before she had given him a son who could inherit the property. That was the argument that your sister's in-laws had used when they forcefully took the plot from her.

Even though your mother and Sisi Memo were not close, she was still sympathetic towards her stepdaughter; a sympathy no doubt born of her understanding of how it felt to be the recipient of unwarranted envy from an affinal family. She had said, in a tone that felt as if someone had lit a fire underneath you, "Let this be the last time that these words come from your mouth, do you hear me?"

You had looked at your mother. She was forty-six but she already looked well in her fifties. The leathery skin that hung on her thin frame had all the tell-tale signs of a life of toiling daily, doing her best to raise five children on the small, sandy patch of land that was your farm and contending with the adversities that came with being the third of your father's wives, the first two having died. There was, in her frailty, in her slouched shoulders and sunken eyes, a woman who had long abandoned any dreams of her own and now lived solely for her children.

"Yes mhamha. I will do as you say." The two of you had looked at each other. In that silence, you hoped she had found the thing inside of you that she had been searching for.

Having lived in the rural area all your life, you were not prepared to navigate the rapid pace and ubiquitous apathy of city life. What little information you had got from your schoolmates who had been fortunate enough to spend some holidays with their relatives in the city had ill equipped you for what you were going to have to endure. The city, with its speeding *kombis,* ceaseless car horns and engines and people whose eyes only looked at where they were going, having no time to exchange a pleasantry and who only ever looked at you to assess whether or not there was anything to be gained from you. You were not ready for the packs of scrawny young men with dry, lewd lips and eyes that stripped parts of you away until you felt naked, who whistled and howled whenever you passed them by. But least of all you were not ready for your sister.

She was a busy woman and made sure to tell you as such the day you arrived. She had a daughter who was studying medicine in China who needed school fees and between working at the high school and in her garden to sell what she could to make ends meet, she had no time for "rubbish." Rubbish, you would soon find out, meant, among other things, seeing you idling around the house. According to her there was always something that needed doing and idleness was a symptom of laziness, the ultimate transgression. "An idle mind is the devil's workshop," she would say. Your sister was as impatient and as unaccommodating as the city. But still, there was, underneath the short temper and sharp words, a woman who had had to grow accustomed to doing what needed to be done with the utmost of subsistence. Courtesy was a form of indulgence that she simply had no time for.

Having already been berated for watching TV, which according to her ought to be done only after the last meal of the day had been had and the dishes washed, you were relieved when schools finally opened. You finally had something to do during the day other than working with your sister in her garden.

Your respite was short-lived. In addition to a curriculum that was more challenging and demanding, you had to contend with teachers who taught rashly, eager only to finish their syllabi on time and dispense with their students most of whom were only too happy to leave. They paid no heed to those who were slower at grasping the complexities of algebra or digesting all the profusion of centuries of European history and promptly left them behind. The moment they saw your childlike handwriting and how bad your English was, they discarded you as another lost cause. You tried to talk to your sister about it but she gave you the same advice that, to her, was the solution to every problem: work harder.

So you found yourself overwhelmed and alone, a world away from the assuring familiarity of home, from smoke flavoured conversations with your mother, living a life that always seemed too far ahead of you. Until you met Nyasha.

He did not have that look of the other city boys that left you bare and vulnerable. Instead, his eyes, dark and shielded by a pair of thick rimmed spectacles, were reassuring and comforting. He was in the same class as you at High 1.

Never bereft of a cheery smile or something to say, it took a short time for him to become your friend and for that friendship to blossom into something more. There was something familiar in how he always inquired after your family or your day, the way you were used to in the village. He was eager to help you with your schoolwork but more often than not, when he spoke you felt lost in his voice, uplifted and thrust in the warm past and the promising future.

Although he did his best to help you, the village education system had left you too far behind, and you struggled with things that he retorted, sometimes with a hint of frustration, you should not have been struggling with. He was patient, however, and his explanations were the closest you got to understanding, but it was still all too much. When you sat for your O levels you hoped for the best, but the eight-letter long chain of D's and E's on your results sheet came as no surprise. That still did little to curb the feeling of disappointment, further aggravated by your sister's unabashed displeasure. You tried again the next year and did slightly better with two C's. It raised your hopes for the next year despite your sister saying she could not afford to keep sending you to school, so you had to study from home and then register for the exams. It was a fair enough compromise, the only drawback being that you could no longer enjoy your walks back home with Nyasha. You tried to make up for that by occasionally sneaking him into the house when you knew your sister would be arriving late. It was these occasions that eventually led to your current predicament.

"How was your day *sisi*?" Your sister did not look at you as she answered, her eyes instead landing on the open pot on the stove.

"My day was well if yours was well. *Ko* what happened?" She did not sound angry. She sounded tired. The dread that you had been feeling slowly gave way to guilt. The response that you had rehearsed when you expected apprehension was suddenly unusable and your tongue could not fashion a new one quickly enough. You hung your head in silence.

You still do not know why you did not simply tell her the truth, that you had been vomiting in the toilet when you burnt the pot.

Now as you lie on the floor, you wish that you had. Things could have turned out differently.

Instead, you chose to confide in Mai Gamu. You met her later that evening on your way to buy *matemba* from the supermarket. Naturally, she wanted to know what had happened and the eventual resolution between you and your sister.

It was easy enough, with that faux concern of hers, to make you feel as if she was someone you could open up to. You told her that you had not been feeling well, constantly feeling nauseated and fatigued. You had thought nothing of it, thinking that maybe you had eaten some food that had been about to turn. You had not even considered the possibility of pregnancy. That was until she asked when you had last had your period. You were not quite sure but it was certainly more than a month ago, perhaps two.

Your first thought was how you would tell your mother. Would she be able to bear the weight of her disappointment? And then there was your sister. If she reacted the way she did to some of the minor offences that you had committed, you could only imagine what she would do to you for this. In the space of that single question, your world that had been lingering on the periphery of collapse, all of a sudden came crashing down.

Mai Gamu was quick to offer her help. She could get you something that could "sort it all out." You were too relieved to even consider the possibility of complications, too naïve. All you felt was gratitude when three days later, you took the small pack of herbs that she gave you and listened to the instructions that she gave you diligently.

Now as you lie on the toilet floor, blood oozing from between your legs and your stomach being torn apart, you think back to that night with your mother, about the thing inside you that she thought you did not have and a lone tear rolls down your face.

Secondhand Emotion

There were three of us. There was Simba, who was my best friend at that time, whom I saw yesterday at the corner of Robert Mugabe and First Street, leaning against the brick wall on the southern side of Spar supermarket, his head jerking intermittently from side to side as if he was looking for trouble. I found out later from Rudo, his brother's ex-girlfriend, that he was a *change money*, trading foreign currency illegally on the black market. I always saw him doing something with money. Like stock trading or brokering. He had the head of an entrepreneur.

He was just as tall as I remembered, towering a good head or two above the rest of the crowd so that he was easy to spot. He was also hard to evade. Before I could turn on my heels and walk the other way, he saw me and waved. I walked towards him wearing what I hoped was a convincing imitation of a smile that felt itchy on my face, like I was wearing the woollen monkey hat that my mother used to make me wear during my childhood winters, that covered everything but my eyes. We shook hands, slapped each other's back and said, "*Madii?*"

Then there was Kudzi. She and I had one thing in common: we were afraid of being alone. We were haunted by any emptinesses around us or perhaps especially, by the threat of them. I haven't seen her for two years now, a year less than I had not seen Simba before our unplanned meeting yesterday. I haven't spoken to her for a little less than that. We stayed in touch after I ended things with her. I have a habit of clinging to things that I have broken. She is a victim of her hope. At least she did when we were still together. The kind of hope that does not extinguish when it ought to, so that it eventually singes everything to disappointment and despair. I heard also from Rudo that she is still talking to Simba. She never stopped even when we were together and I always hated that. I wondered yesterday if he knew that I knew, and if so, how he felt about it. Did he feel triumphant? Or some bitter sense of satisfaction?

Me, I lived in the future. It haunted me, collected overhead, on the horizon like the gathering of rain clouds, dark and looming, on the verge of something turbulent. You see, I was always alone in that future. So, I made sure I was never alone in the present. I was always running away from this lonely future, but it seemed every step I took to get away from it, it only got closer. That is why I loved Kudzi. She and I were perfect for each other. We filled the haunted caverns of each other's empty spaces, saved each other from the places our minds went when the world felt too hollow and unkind for our frail dreams.

When I saw Simba yesterday, memories of our time together in university rushed back like torrential rain, pouring relentlessly on the barren place where I kept the things I wished to forget, uncovering the shallow unmarked grave where I had managed to bury the things from the past that I had no use remembering.

At the time, that time when it was the three of us, we were… our characters were crude and volatile things, defined more than anything else by what we felt and desired, rather than any consideration for factors outside of ourselves and the stringy reach and inevitability of consequence.

Simba was the kind of person who believed they could overcome and accomplish anything in life using nothing more than their god given wits. A tall, scrawny boy whose intelligence had managed to pluck him, overnight, from the dusty rural areas of Masvingo and dropped him in a university in Cyprus, his conceitedness was, if not tolerable, then at least understandable. He had that air about him of a person who had been a prefect in high school, as if he stood on higher ground than everyone else. He had been the headboy actually, at Pamushana High. He was handsome, in a sun beaten, weathered way so that you didn't notice it until you had looked at him for a while. And he had a disregard for his physical appearance that could effortlessly announce itself even amongst a crowd of four hundred plus university freshmen that had just arrived in a new country for the first time. He aroused in me the feeling of the long dry season after the harvest, the smell of a cattle kraal, the languor of a remote village in the late afternoon.

Kudzi held your gaze when you talked to her so that you could not help falling into the dark pools of her eyes, could not help being trapped by them and her voice came out like a song from the bottom of their obsidian, sun speckled depths. When she laughed, she always closed her eyes and threw her head back and you could see that all her wisdom teeth had been removed. The first time I saw her was at a birthday party held on the rooftop of our apartment building, for one of the residents, a shy girl called Ropafadzo who wore spectacles kind beads in her hair. That first time, I couldn't help but notice her. She had short hair, dyed a conspicuous bright pink, front teeth that were a little too large and skin that shimmered in the glow of the braai fire like dark satin. Simba was with her. They spent the entirety of that night standing together in a corner on the rooftop, drinking, laughing and flirting.

If Kudzi's mother hadn't died, I don't think she and Simba would have ever ended up together. The two of them were a mismatch. Simba was pragmatic, mathematical. He had the annoying habit of seeing everything as either a problem or a solution, an option or an alternative which always left me feeling as if I wasn't intelligent enough. Kudzi on the other hand, was a collection of the things she felt, always reacting, through one emotion or other, to the world around her. That's not to say they were a bad couple. On the contrary, the sad circumstances that brought them together made their bond that much stronger. I'm only saying, it wouldn't have happened if Kudzi's mother hadn't died.

Shortly after we arrived in Cyprus, she received news that her mother was very sick. Her mother was her lone remaining parent after her father had died in a car accident when she was nine. When her relatives eventually fessed up and told her the truth, that her mother had really died but they could not afford to buy her a plane ticket, they had already buried her mother and had the funeral without her. She cried herself hollow until she lost her voice. She didn't eat or bath for two whole days until Simba cooked and convinced her to eat half a packet of Indomie noodles. After that, he didn't leave her side until she was ready to face the world again. Well, at least until she couldn't put it off any longer. Only pieces of her came back from the place that her grief took her.

Simba was ok with it at first. He never allowed himself to feel the burden of her. But then, these things go the way that they go, and he got tired of it all after a while. But not before I'd seen enough of it, the two of them seemingly tangled in each other, living two ends of the same life, that a feeling, not quite envy, because it was not so nebulous, but a close cousin to it, had been stirred inside me.

I had more than my fair share of relationships. And that was precisely the problem. I spent too much time around Simba and Kudzi, around their love and their story, to evade the need to compare myself to them, what they shared, and it came to be that anything I had felt like a husk, like what their relationship would leave if it were to shed the superficial pleasures, the façade of perfection for the benefit of onlookers.

Kudzi started to become the embodiment of what I was lacking. It was the summer that Simba started working. He got a job as a hotel cleaner in another city so he was often gone for the entire week and would only come back on weekends. Because we had got so used to spending time together, the three of us, Kudzi and I continued to do so in his absence. Even when Simba was around but was too tired because of work, she and I would be together. It was innocent at first. And then small thoughts, nocent daydreams and what ifs started to buzz around my head like flies around a turd. The big one, the green bomber, was the thought, that if her mother hadn't died then she and Simba would not be together, and it buzzed and buzzed so loud, I couldn't unhear it.

Simba confided in me that he had grown tired of her. He no longer had room to breathe, he said. She had gone from being a solution to a problem. I tried to find comfort in that, tugged at it with wretched desperation and pulled it apart but there was nothing in there to assuage my guilt, the feeling of wanting to betray my friend which in itself felt like a betrayal. All I could do was swallow my feelings. But these things are not so easily hidden. *Rina manyanga hariputirwe –* You cannot conceal something that has horns.

The whispers started to follow us quickly enough. The ones that come from the shadows that you never know whose lips they came from and when you reach out to try and find the source, you are bitten on the hand. We were a boy and a girl spending so much time together and it was foolish of me to think that no one would take notice, that there could be such a thing as innocent love, that love even had anything to do with it.

Kudzi was crying the day she came and told me that Simba had said he was not ok with us spending time together anymore, that if she continued to do so, that would be the end for them. I'd never seen her cry before. When she cried she seemed to shrink. I would see her cry a lot later on. The last time I saw her, she was crying too.

The fact that Simba did not come to me himself told me all I needed to know about what had become of our friendship. I was angry. I was angry at the people who could not mind their own business, but mostly for the fact that they had seen through me. I was angry too at Simba, for having so easily listened to them and turned on me, for trying to take away Kudzi, what she meant to me, not even because he wanted her but because he could not stand the thought of having her taken from him, not while everybody watched. It made no difference to me that Kudzi had refused to listen to him, that she was willing to remain my friend even at the risk of losing their relationship.

Anger is like a blunt tool propelled by an unstoppable force. It can beat anything down and turn it into resentment. And this resentment is not always directed towards the right people.

My anger was directed at Simba, but my resentment was at Kudzi. For not having seen what she did to me, how helpless she left me. For making me dream impossible dreams that tasted so bitter they made my eyes water. I was insulted that she even needed to choose between the two of us considering how hard I had fallen for her. For days, weeks afterwards, I couldn't rid myself of the reek of the injustices that often plague an enamoured heart.

I taught myself to hate her. It was the only way I could accept the way things were, the only way to let go of what could have been. But if I am being honest with myself, all I could manage was a few lethargic plumes of smoke. I could never truly ignite my hatred; have it burn as fierce as it did for Simba. It was lukewarm, tepid, sleepy so that sometimes, a lot of times, I forgot that it was there at all, until I really looked for it. You cannot hold smoke in your hands, it will just slip through your fingers.

A year passed. I convinced myself that I had moved on with my life. I searched for the thing I'd almost had with Kudzi, thinking maybe I had it somewhere on me in a hidden pocket, but she had taken all of it with her. That lonely future was licking at my heels and I could sense it like those undefined shapes in the dark that are always a hair away from touching your skin. Anything I had once felt for Kudzi had dissolved into memory.

I had moved away from the apartment where she and Simba lived, for my peace of mind. And then Simba stopped coming to classes. At first, I thought that he was ill, which I lost no sleep over, but after two weeks, I decided to go to the old apartment under the guise of looking for Rudo, who, at that time was still his brother's girlfriend. He had dropped out of school and gone back home. Of course he had. Apparently, he had had some luck in sports betting and he was going to start some business or other. Kudzi had stayed behind.

Our friendship, I later realised, had not died as I had wanted to believe, but simply withered, like a flower waiting to be watered. We almost picked up where we had left off. She was still together with Simba, but now, with the distance between them, the threat of me gone, they were starting to crumble.

I didn't mean to rekindle the things between us that had already been burnt to ash. I simply missed my friend. And with Simba gone, we were free to be what we had once been, to turn our heads from the past and start anew. It was all I wanted. Simba must have felt the same way, must have understood that she needed a friend, because he didn't fuss over our renewed relationship. If he felt anything other than that, he didn't show it and I didn't care.

I had learned from my mistake and was careful to make sure that I did not repeat it. I boarded up the spaces that I had once foolishly thought that only Kudzi could fill. But while I was busy doing so, I forgot that her spaces were wide open, that I could just as easily fill them for *her*.

You do not refuse a gift that has been offered to you twice. I remember the day that she called Simba to tell him about us. It was the second time I saw her crying. He disappeared quietly, like a morning star. The haunted future went away and there was sunshine and summer.

But you know the way these things go.

I don't know how Simba felt about all that happened, didn't want to know.

That was until I saw him yesterday in the city centre. I asked him. He did this thing … he looked far away, like he was searching for something from a long time ago and I don't know whether he found it or not but all he said was, "It was so long ago. I don't remember, and if I did, it wouldn't matter."

"That is so," I said. He was right.

"True," he said. And then he asked me, "What happened to the two of you?"

"The way these things go. You can't run from it."

He had a look about him that was more than just the passage of time. Like … like he had grown something inside of him, something too fundamental that could only be diminished by being named.

I confessed to him, "There was never a haunted future." I wanted him to know how wrong I had been.

"Huh?" But he didn't understand.

"Nothing."

I asked him also, because I really needed to know, because I'm not so sure any more about any of what happened, "Did you love her?"

"Who?" I looked at him. I could see his mathematical head at work. After some time he said, "What did love have to do with it?" And I was impressed again by his intelligence.

We stood together for a while, but the past could not bring us together. We are now strangers, but perhaps that's alright. We said our goodbyes and went our separate ways.

Jagged Pieces

I always imagined that gigs, our collaborated high school dances with our sister school, St. Dominic's, were a rather cruel enterprise, meant to determine where one stood on our high school's somewhat derogative social hierarchy. That they were compulsory only exacerbated that fact. It was an affair fuelled by our need as teenagers to fit in; to be as inconspicuous as possible in a coerced game of hide and never be seen by being extraordinary at being ordinary, meant to show who could or couldn't talk to girls which, being an all boy's school, was pivotal in determining those of us who "had swagger" as we called it, and those who did not. Having swagger was essentially a golden pass for virtually everything. You were automatically spared scrutiny on all the other minuscule shortcomings that people were mocked for. It no longer mattered how poorly you did in school. Or what kind of car your family drove. Or how ugly you or your sister who came on Visiting Sundays was. And paradoxically, it also no longer mattered if you didn't talk to girls. If high school taught me anything, it's that the combination of those pesky, notorious raging hormones and the toxicity of – pardonne mon Français – several hundred swinging dicks, is never conducive to anything good.

I hated gigs. I hated the theatricality of them. Boys donning the most overpowering of their cheap body spray, scrambling to talk to girls whose personalities were buried so deep under their coy one-word answers that they were probably bioluminescent, all in full view of everyone – just so we could keep score – most of whom made little to no effort to be even moderately interesting because for them the achievement was simply to be approached. I did have other reasons. But this is not to say I didn't participate in this theatre of Axes and Bruts; Sunday bests that only once a month, were spotless, the white shirts dazzling and the grey slacks with creases that could cut the stale bread we had for breakfast; and conversations shallower only than the malleable personalities of the teenagers who partook in them.

The ones who were unable to converse with the fairer sex we labelled as *mabhenzo*. Of course there were several, and a lot of them did a decent job of hiding it, or at the very least, staying out of the spotlight well enough that it didn't cause them too many problems except when we compiled our monthly, post gig lists of the top ten or sometimes twenty *mabhenzo*, but there were five notable ones. Each member of the quintet was known for a different reason, but what united them was the fact that at every gig, these wanna-be renegades would gather somewhere and talk amongst themselves, refusing to give in to the pressure to participate in our circus of hay fever triggering conversations and trying to outdance each other back in the days of the now defunct 'dougie', one of the ever changing trends from the perpetually innovative US of A-holes that made it to our African shores via the YouTube boat and the similarly short-lived 'clarks', which, in contrast, were a homegrown fad that every ghetto – Chi-town, Fio, Mbare et al. – tried to patent. If it were a different place and a different time, I would have admired them. But it wasn't. I was a member of the collective, a part of the system, as cemented in its workings as our cheap deodorants, and I had to play my part and 'see' them for what they truly were. *Mabhenzo.*

The most notorious of them was Nyasha, His Excellency, the president of all *mabhenzo,* the pioneer of zero fucks. At one gig – we must have been form two's then – he took some chairs and built a miniature fort around himself near the entrance of the school hall where our gigs were held, inside which he then proceeded to sit until it was time to leave. He was especially peculiar and, I thought, always trying a little too hard to show how little he cared about what people thought of him with such performances, which incidentally always drew more attention to him.

Then there was Abacar, the skinny, and famously well-endowed Mozambican. At an inter-division swimming tournament, his swim trunks had come down as he was getting out of the pool, displaying his eminent member to the entire school. Even shrunken from the cold water, it was still quite impressive; a spectacle to behold and the staff of legends (yes, you read that correctly) and it had earned him the nickname Skinny D.

There was Darlington and Tadiwa who were best friends from primary school and the most pretentious people in the entire school. Inseparable, they eerily resembled each other, both fat, with stupidly rich families; the kind that spent holidays overseas while the rest of us were sent off to our obscure villages to herd cattle and help our grandparents with farming or harvesting, depending on the season; both wearing glasses probably because they spent so much time on their PlayStation 3's or their fancy sliding phones with QWERTY keyboards; and both speaking with exaggerated American accents about comic books and alternative music and science fiction in poorly disguised attempts to be as unAfrican as possible, or dare I say even, unBlack.

Lastly, there was Ralph, the smartest and most reserved person in our form. A quiet enigma, he only spoke when spoken to and was a regular receiver of the Merit badges which were awarded to the students with the most outstanding academic performances at the beginning of each term. Three were displayed proudly on his immaculate green blazer as he sat quietly, listening to the group.

That day they'd chosen to sit next to the piano that was placed at the back of the school hall during the gigs. Kupa was sitting close to them, pretending to read a novel. I could tell because he'd been reading the same page for almost ten minutes.

Kupa was my secret boyfriend. *(What? A boyfriend? Aren't you a boy? This is the twenty-first century. If you insist on the offensiveness of it all, I suggest you send a strongly worded prayer to upper management. Ha!)* So I knew that he pretended to read in order not to draw attention to himself. He loved reading fantasy novels and Greek mythology – when he was actually reading. He hated religion, teenagers and soccer, exactly in that order. He was impeccable, which was later used as 'proof' against him at our kangaroo court. And he was a social outcast, too much of an aberration to be considered one of us and therefore to be part of our system. He didn't even bother trying to speak to girls. He couldn't have, even if he wanted to.

For that, he had Blazerboy to thank. Blazerboy was – and in the minds of some of us, still is – the terror and resident bully of our stream, not because of what he could do to you physically, but due to his exceptional ability to manipulate the hive of our gullible, adolescent minds. He caught on early enough how to exploit our pliability to his advantage, elevating or humiliating any person with a well-timed quip here, an elaborate matinee there, and more often than not, choosing to do the latter. He could easily make or break a person with the right words, and he took no small pleasure in doing so. Unfortunately for Kupa, he broke him, in more ways than one. He started the rumour that Kupa was gay.

It all started with a picture of Adam Lambert that fell out of Kupa's pillow – ever impeccable – as he was making his bed one day. Unlike the rest of us who simply straightened out our bedcovers, only to have our housemaster, the obsessive compulsive Mr G, make us redo them on the days that he chose to do his impromptu inspections, Kupa always *made* his bed, from the mattress protector all the way to the duvet, fluffing his pillows and changing the covers on a weekly basis. The picture was a gift from me; a tease after he'd told me he had a crush on the singer. Sentimental as he was, he'd kept the damned thing, knowing full well what would probably happen if anyone ever saw it. I'm not saying he had it coming, but he could have been a little more careful. But that's all spilt milk now. After Blazerboy's discovery, by the time classes started two hours later that morning, the story was that Blazerboy had caught Kupa in the toilet stall, masturbating to the picture. By the end of the day, revised and extended editions were already circulating the grapevine which included an offer to fellate Blazerboy in an effort to persuade him to keep his discovery a secret. A few weeks later, when the term ended, sequels and spinoffs were already being distributed not only around our campus but to other schools as well – accusations that Kupa had made several advances on some students, peeked on several of them in toilet stalls and groped several more in the showers.

On more than one occasion Kupa had had to walk into the classroom to find obscene sketches of men intertwined in complex, usually distasteful but always imaginative sexual configurations, one labelled with his name, the other Adam Lambert's. It goes without saying that I was abhorred by the abuse, but I couldn't deny the wit and the ingenuity that was put into some of the 'art'. Kupa never asked me who the perpetrators were and I was content to hold my tongue.

His next run-in with Blazerboy came one morning, when he woke up to find Blazerboy poking his rear with a broomstick, the rest of our dorm mates cheering and laughing including the dorm prefect who had come to wake us up. There were several more similar incidents that Kupa endured at Blazerboy's hands, each more antipathetic than the last, but he refused to let him have the satisfaction of showing him how much these things hurt him, always feigning indifference.

It was these incidents that played in my head as I wove my way towards Kupa and the quintet, through the stuffy crowd of swagger haves and have-nots. I was feeling particularly guilty after I noticed Kupa looking up several times from his pretend reading and seeing me chatting up a girl whose name I'd forgotten before the end of our conversation. When I reached them, I lingered around the quintet for a short while, nodding along to their conversation about the new Iron Man movie which, unsurprisingly, was led by the dynamic duo of our resident unAfrican Africans, all the while trying to avoid meeting his eyes. I was the paranoid half of our relationship. After what I thought was a sufficiently discreet amount of time had passed, I announced loudly that I was going to the toilet and left, glancing once behind me to ensure that Kupa had got the message.

Our dorms were usually deserted during gigs. The ones among us who'd long accepted that they would never leave their place at the bottom of the coolness ladder usually hid in the TV room, safe from the occasional patrols of Mr G who, in paradoxical contrast to his lectures about how girls were no more than seductresses meant to deter our focus from books and "being good boys," was insistent that some occasional socialising with the opposite sex "would keep thoughts of any kind of mischief out of our heads." And I'm not certain of it, but I always thought he would look at Kupa when he said this. The dorms would be closed for the day, only to be opened after the last St Dominic's bus had departed, leaving us behind to revisit and replay the events of the day for an entire month until the next gig, but more importantly to reassess and reorganise the social rankings based on an infallible algorithm with such variables as number of girls spoken to, duration of conversations, any exchange of memorabilia such as notes or gifts, etc. There were self-appointed individuals whose job it was to keep a record of all this without whose hard work and dedication, the healthy and proper social development of many of us would not have been prematurely derailed. However, in a rare instance of communal solidarity, some enterprising students had figured out a way to unlock the door from the outside with the help of a knife and a clothes hanger – which thenceforth were kept in the small hedge leading up to the dormitory door – and had been kind enough to share their discovery with the rest of us. It was after we had all got tired of Mr G, a dangerously excitable man, sometimes locking it when he came to do his breakfast time inspections for any dissenters who chose not to attend the most important meal of the day. The technique was employed on many occasions, most commonly during Sunday mass, but gigs were not amongst them. Even if one did not attend for the primary objective of this very special event, one could always bear witness to those who did, which was always a priceless contribution in the sustenance of our fucked up little microcosm.

Deserted dorm meant deserted beds. Privacy. Opportunity. Kupa and I made do with our stolen moments in toilet stalls, but the anxiety I got from those encounters often nullified what little intimacy we were able to salvage in the confines of the literally shitty and more importantly, thin walls of the toilet cubicles.

So we made our way to the dorms.

The thing I've learned about opportunity since that day though, is that it is rarely ever seen by only one person.

Kupa was just beginning to zip my trousers back up. I was lying on the bed, spent, still savouring the last fragments of the orgasm I'd just had that still lingered in the tips of my fingers. So if you walked in on us at that very moment you would have seen me, lying on the bed, my eyes closed, looking like I was sleeping and Kupa, the rumoured class homo, kneeling next to my bed, his hands on the open zipper of my trousers. If you were a bully that took pride in twisting facts for your amusement and had a pre-existing bone to pick with someone who seemed impervious to your slander, you would have seen a faggot, about to molest me while I was sleeping, ashen with shock.

When I heard Blazerboy's voice, something inside me collapsed. So readily, in fact, that I realised that I'd been waiting for it to do just that all along. I remained still, dazed by the sheer abruptness of our predicament. It was those few precious moments that I lay frozen, willing violently to wake up from what my brain kept insisting was a bad dream, that inadvertently 'saved' me. Kupa, on the other hand, jerked up and Blazerboy, having already made up his mind about that moment months before it came, interpreted this action as an admission of guilt. "Only a thief runs when they are discovered." Blazerboy later said that to Mr G, when he came to break up our kangaroo court that we had later that day, where among other things, several students 'confessed' how Kupa had tried to do the same to them while they were sleeping. Strangely, each testimony always ended with the victims waking up before anything untoward had been done to them and not a single one explained why they hadn't come forward before.

I opened my eyes. Five familiar faces stood at the door, a few feet behind Blazerboy. Their faces conveyed their Ahs and WTFs clearly enough for their mouths which were covered by their hands. I looked slowly from them to Kupa. He just knelt there, limp, not knowing what to do. Even though he did his best to maintain his usual impassive face, the fear in his eyes was unmistakable.

"*Ngaarohwe!*" Later, at the disciplinary hearing, I learned that it was Abacar who said it. It was an invitation, a call to action. They had borne witness to a sick perversion and the only way they knew to deal with it was to beat it away. Like I said, raging hormones and swinging dicks. Blazerboy took one step towards us and then another, each one more purposeful than the one before and each one making the bile rise higher in my throat. I closed my eyes and braced myself.

I heard the first blow. And then a second that was followed by a throaty sound that conjured images in my mind of an animal dying. Then the blows started raining. Eventually, I dared myself to open my eyes. Kupa was somewhere on the floor surrounded by the six boys, all clamouring to deliver a blow. No one was paying any attention to me. Slowly the realisation of what was happening dawned on me. If shame alone could make up for what I did, then I would say that I was ashamed of what I felt. I would say, all serious like and looking at my toes, and looking like a disgraced politician charged with corruption, "I'm ashamed to say that, buoyed by my instinct for self-preservation, from the abundant spectrum of human emotion, what I felt in that moment, of all the things I could – should – have felt..." But shame isn't enough here. It doesn't absolve me. So I'm just going to say what I felt and you can judge me at your own leisure. I felt relieved.

It was only a moment. Yet its bounds have gone beyond the brief instant of time that it occurred, spreading like mould from that temporal nova up to today, haunting me, gnawing at me in my most vulnerable moments and prompting me to tell this story. I've had time to try and convince myself that it was my imagination, that it was a rush of adrenaline or that I was confused and in shock. But the thing is, I can't ever forget the look in his eyes. I can still see it as vividly as if I was looking at a picture. A bloodied and bruised face. Those eyes said one thing no matter how I look at it. "Help me." And I knew. I was disgusted with myself even before I made my decision. I knew even before I looked away, that I wasn't going to.

When Kupa's mother came and screamed in front of Mr G's house, beating her chest and spitting on the ground, I detected a slight desperation underneath her theatrics. A desperation that, perhaps suggested that her anger was not completely directed at the housemaster or even at the boys that had beaten her gay son. Still, she succeeded in getting Blazerboy expelled. Hasta la Vista, baby. A good riddance! The quintet got off with a stern talking to and a lecture from our school priest about the dangers of "deviant acts that were against the laws of God." I stuck to the story that I was sleeping when everything happened because I hadn't been feeling well. I was given a week long hiatus from school "to deal with my trauma and heal." The school and Kupa's parents agreed that it was in their mutual interest that news of the incident was not made public. In return for their silence, Kupa was to be allowed to continue at the school. But none of us were surprised when he didn't show up on the opening day of the following school term.

I'll admit, I was hurt but not surprised when I realised, after I sent him a series of half-hearted apology texts that all went unread, that he had blocked me. I told myself countless times that I would visit him in the hospital, apathetic promises borne of contrition rather than concern and I knew I wouldn't, even as I said them. Underneath my guilt, as I beat myself with the stick of hindsight, I couldn't escape a niggling sense of solace that I was spared from having to see him again, having to come up with an explanation or worse still, having to apologise. I knew that I had broken something between us and I would only cut myself if I attempted to put the jagged pieces back together. It was easier that way.

A Text Thread

[15/06, 18:09] Anesu: Not so quiet anymore huh? I almost couldn't get you to stop talking today. If I hadn't been in a rush you would have made me deaf *ka* 😂😂

[15/06, 19:01] CeeTheScribe: Lol. Yeah, thankfully I grew out of that

[15/06, 19:01] CeeTheScribe: Man, it's been forever

[15/06, 19:05] Anesu: I kind of liked the old you. You were so mysterious and sombre. Ahh remember that time in class when that guy – I can't remember his name – pronounced sombre as som-bray kkkk

[15/06, 19:06] Anesu: It has hasn't it? God, I was really happy to see you today. I needed to see a friendly old face

[15/06, 19:06] CeeTheScribe: I literally cringe when I think about those days. I think I was as emo as you could get in Zimbabwe without being called a Satanist. And I think the guy was Tadiwa lol. It feels like another lifetime

[15/06, 19:07] CeeTheScribe: Me too. When I saw you, I realised how much I missed you

[15/06, 19:07] Anesu: Yeah, I get you

[15/06, 19:08] CeeTheScribe: So … you've changed

[15/06, 19:09] Anesu: Oh, you noticed that kkkk. Yeah life decided to give me a makeover lol

[15/06, 19:10] CeeTheScribe: 🤣 I see you still have your terrible sense of humour. So tell me, what's been going on with you?

[15/06, 19:12] **Anesu**: *Aiwawo* shut up. We both know you liked me for it

[15/06, 19:12] **Anesu**: God, I don't even know where to start

[15/06, 19:13] **CeeTheScribe**: You could start where you disappeared on me

[15/06, 19:14] **Anesu**: Ok fair enough. I deserve that. I'm sorry for not staying in touch but you have to understand Craig. There was a lot going on with me at the time and I just … I was having a hard time coping and I ended up shutting people off.

[15/06, 19:15] **CeeTheScribe**: You could have reached out Nesu. If not at the time then after. Didn't I deserve at least that much?

[15/06, 19:16] **Anesu**: Of course you did. And I'm sorry. I can't tell you how sorry I am.

[15/06, 19:16] **CeeTheScribe**: It's fine. Tell me, what was going on with you then?

[15/06, 19:17] **Anesu**: It's been hard Craig, I'm not going to lie to you. My life has just been going down a slope forever now and I'm doing everything I can to try to hang on but haa… And I've been all alone and I can't even talk to anyone about it because there isn't anyone. But you were always a good listener. This is going to be really long but I just need to tell someone. Sorry but I've just wanted to talk to someone for so long. I don't want to burden you or anything. You don't even have to read everything I type, but

I just need to say it you know. I need to let it out because it's eating me up

[15/06, 19:19] CeeTheScribe: It's ok. Talk to me

[15/06, 19:23] Anesu: Oh God, I feel so emotional just thinking about this. I know you always liked your fucked up stories. This is going to be a good one. Ok so it all started when my mom passed away. But before I get to that, let me tell you about this boy. His name is Tinashe. Actually … I have so much to say, so I'm going to write this like a book, kind of. Maybe you can put this in one of your books when you finally become a published author like you always wanted.

[15/06, 1924] CeeTheScribe: Yeah, sure. Do that

[15/06, 19:39] Anesu: This first part is called Love. When people say the devil will come as an angel of light *ka*, they are not lying. So what happened is some time after you left, maybe a year and a half, I met this guy at uni. He was an accounting student too, but he was in his fourth year. I thought he was alright you know. He wasn't like one of those stupid boys who say I love you the day you give them your number and start calling you their beautiful queen every day when they send you their good morning text alongside their dick pic. He was sweet and a little shy. Come to think of it, he was a bit like you. But more … expressive. He would give me notes and we had discussions together and things like that. He didn't even seem interested in me at the beginning so obviously I fell for him. I fell hard Craig. I became one of those stupid girls who giggles at everything he says even if it's not that funny. I smiled like an idiot at his text messages. I even started talking less with

other boys just for his sake even though we weren't dating. I
texted him almost every day and the days that I didn't took
a lot of self-restraint because I didn't want him to think I
was needy. I started wearing nicer clothes when I knew I
was going to see him. Haa I was in love my guy. Head over
heels. I had dreams about him. I fantasized about what it
would be like to make love to him. That's even how I
thought of it. Not having sex. Not fucking. No, we would
make love. But those were just daydreams. I never really
wanted to do anything with him. But I wasn't going to give
him the satisfaction of telling him how I felt, so I waited.
And I waited and I waited and I waited. And I waited some
more. Then finally, he asked me out. I was on cloud nine
that day. I asked him why it took him so long since I so
obviously liked him. He said he wanted to see how much
deeper he could fall for me before asking me out but he
realized he wasn't going to ever stop falling. I know it was
cheesy but it got me *amana*. He was like that. Always saying
the things I wanted to hear until eventually I just wanted to
hear whatever he said. So we started going out. He never
asked for sex or anything. It was fucking great. He was
great. I felt great. That was just the calm before the storm.

[15/06, 20:16] **Anesu**: This next part is called Despair.
Mhamha died. I don't even really know what happened. I
am not superstitious but some of the things make me think
that maybe there was something unnatural about what
happened. Other people think so too. The word witchcraft
was said a few times after she got sick. She just started
having these headaches out of nowhere. Like she would
wake up in the middle of the night screaming. I was a 2.2 in
uni at the time and I stayed on campus but I had to come

back home to take care of her. My useless brother was too busy "hustling" even though he had nothing to show for it. If hustling meant stealing and getting girls pregnant then sure, that's what he was doing. In any case, Mhamha didn't want anything to do with him. My little sister was only in form 1 at the time. Mhamha's sister helped a little but her husband refused to let her come and stay with us. So I was the only one left. *Iwe* it was really bad Craig. She started losing weight. I think every day she lost like a kilogram or something because hai … And she wouldn't eat. The little that she did, she threw up. First, she had trouble travelling long distances because she always came back feeling so tired and she just passed out, so she stopped going to work. Then she had trouble walking from her room to the kitchen. Then she couldn't stand at all. We only had enough money to go to a public hospital which is as useful as going to a traditional healer in this country. Which we also did by the way. At first, the doctors said it was migraines. Then they told us she was just overworked and needed to rest. It was nonsense because my mother had been working since before I was born and this had never happened. Then they said it was malaria but they didn't have the medicine. I realised that we were just wasting our money going back. I asked my aunt in the UK for money so we could take her to a private hospital, but she said things were tough for her too and there was nothing she could do. We tried the church. I don't even know how many pastors came to our house. They spoke in tongues until their voices got hoarse and their suits were drenched in sweat and their veins threatened to burst out of their necks. They threw themselves to the ground as if they were the ones that were possessed. My mother was forced to kneel, her head was jabbed and prodded as if she was being scolded for being sick. After that, my uncle, Bamudiki Baba Paul suggested we look for a traditional healer. I don't believe in that shit but what other choice did I have. So the guy came with his bones and charms and animal skin clothes. He chanted and cried to the ancestors and gave my mother some weird bitter herbs that she could barely swallow. He danced around our house and placed mysterious objects wrapped in white cloth and black cloth and red cloth in obscure corners in the house. Then he asked for his payment before he could remove whatever witchcraft had been sent to "eat" my mother. A week passed, but Mhamha did not get better. A week passed that I had to wipe the shit off her and clean the vomit on her sheets. I had to pinch my nose when I walked into her room because of the nauseating smell of vomit and shit and sickness and herbs left by the witchdoctor. I can still smell it. I could never get that smell out of my nose Craig. A week passed where I cried myself to sleep every night, where my sister and I prayed for hours until my knees hurt and my head ached. I pleaded with God. I demanded. I commanded. I asked why me. But there was no answer Craig. I was in a trance, wondering why God would do this to us. Mhamha was a good woman. I was good. My sister was good. The three of us went to church every Sunday. If anyone deserved punishment it was my brother. He was a good for nothing thief. I didn't even feel guilty thinking that.

About three weeks later my uncle brought a *muporofita*. He came with his shiny bald head and thick beard and white robes and *muteuro* or holy water or whatever it's called. It should only be called useless because that's what it was. He threw away the charms left by the witchdoctor and said that you cannot fight the devil with the devil. He sang his songs and sprayed the house with his holy water. And then, of course, he asked for his payment before he said the prayer that would chase the demons away. Mhamha died three days later.

[15/06, 20:24] **CeeTheScribe**: Oh my God. Anesu I'm so sorry. Why didn't you ever tell me any of this? Now I feel like a dick for complaining about you disappearing. I should have tried to reach out more. Fuck, I'm so sorry I don't even know what to say

[15/06, 20:50] **Anesu**: This next part is called Misery and Betrayal. Craig I was broken. I still am to be honest. When I saw my mother in that coffin I was confused. I didn't know who that skeleton was that I was looking at. We buried her skin and her bones and nothing else. But that was not the end of my problems. Since I'd missed most of the semester looking after her, I wasn't prepared to write the final exams. But I couldn't wait and take them the next semester because I didn't even know if I would have the money for school fees by then. Then there was my uncle. Apparently, our house and everything in it now belonged to him. Mhamha had once told me that he tried to marry her after dad died. She told me it was because he wanted the house. He already had a wife and five children and she was older than him by five years. She had refused and that had led to her being hated by everyone from my dad's side of the family, my paternal grandparents, my uncle and my dad's older sister, the one in England. He said he would let us stay in the house but only if we paid rent. Can you believe that bullshit? Rent to live in our own house. And I was still in school so obviously I couldn't afford to pay rent. He said my brother was working and could help out, even though he and everyone else knew that he didn't even live in the house anymore and he had no job. We couldn't go to live with him because he had too many mouths to feed. Our grandparents had wanted nothing to do with us since our father died. They hated Mhamha. Mhamha's sister and her husband rented a single room and they already had two children. So my sister and I had nowhere to live. But I still had a few more weeks that I could stay at the campus. I only needed to find a place for my sister. So, in spite of my anger I had to beg my uncle. I did it right there at the funeral on Mhamha's fresh grave. I did it in front of everyone so it would be harder for him to say no. He only had to take my sister. Only for a short while until I found something. I didn't know what that thing was that I was supposed to find but I had to find it. I threw myself at his feet and cried. It was both grief and desperation. I told him I would do anything. He agreed. Later that night he came into Mhamha's room where I was sleeping. I still think about the way he whispered, "You will do anything?" It makes my skin crawl! Right there! IN MY MOTHER'S ROOM CRAIG! My dead mother's room which still smelled like vomit and shit and death. He didn't even care about all that. The evil in some people *ka* Craig, it's sickening. The lack of shame. Oh my God, thinking about it makes me sick. I didn't tell anyone. Until now. But it doesn't end there. See my brother had come to the funeral. The next morning when I finally had the strength to wake up, he was gone. And so was my phone. That's when I disappeared. Even when I finally got a small *kambudzi* to replace it I didn't have the energy to even talk to people anymore. A few nights later, the house was robbed. I knew it was my brother, but I didn't care anymore. It was no longer my house. I went back to school. I only barely passed the exams thanks to Tinashe who helped me study and let me copy during the exams. Tinashe. My angel. I can't believe how stupid I was.

Men are all the same, you know (sorry not sorry). They come in different colours but at the centre they're all the same: they have no hearts. I was so messed up and so vulnerable. Honestly, I didn't think those days. I couldn't because every time I did, I would see a skeleton in a coffin. The only thing that I had that wasn't the same dull grey as everything else was Tinashe. He was there for me.

One night we were drinking, something I'd started doing regularly, and we started making out. But he didn't stop taking my clothes off when he got to my underwear like we usually did. But I thought, fuck it. I'd already done it anyway so why not do it with him. And what more did I have to lose. So I did it. And I thought it would fill this hole that was growing inside me. Having someone was just better than being alone and I thought if I did this with him then he would never leave me. I was so stupid. But I was also lost and in pain and I was just on autopilot you know. A month later I found out I was pregnant. And that's when I saw the real Tinashe. He denied it. Can you believe that? I was actually surprised and I thought he was joking at first. But no. He didn't know about my uncle. Besides, that had happened almost two months earlier and I'd also taken a pregnancy test. It was his and he knew it but he still denied it. Suddenly he was exactly like those boys that I'd thought he was so much better than. He'd just wanted to use me. But he was so much worse than them because they made their intentions clear upfront. They didn't make any false promises. I suddenly thought there was at least a certain amount of decency in how honest they were. Not this … this manipulation, this calculated coldness. I should have been angry, but all I felt was defeat and tiredness. Still, I didn't have anywhere else to go, so when the semester ended I went to the house where he lived. He wouldn't even let me in. Can you imagine? All the other lodgers looked at me while I banged on his door with these eyes that were full of judgment. They looked at me like I was a prostitute. I screamed and I cried until my head hurt, but that piece of shit just stayed inside. I could even see him. He kept on refusing. Then I decided to go to his parents' house. His mother was furious at *me* and told me to leave. That was the first time I ever thought of killing myself. I didn't have anywhere to go. The closest person to me was treating me like I was some contagious disease. I didn't even have the strength to walk anymore. I just sat at their gate, not even crying because I didn't have the energy. She threatened to call the police and I half hoped she would because at least I would have somewhere to go and sleep. Eventually his dad came from work. I told him what had happened and explained my situation and he took me in his car and drove me to Tinashe's place. He talked to him and I don't know what he said but I could tell he was angry. After he left, Tinashe let me in.

I had a baby girl. No, I HAVE a baby girl. Her name is Ruvimbo. And she is the only reason I survived this next and final part.

[15/06, 21:21] **Anesu**: It's called Surviving. Whatever Tinashe's father said to him made him keep me in that house but it did not stop him making it clear that he didn't want me there. Most days he would leave in the morning

and come back really late at night or sometimes he wouldn't
come back at all. When he did come, I could smell the sex
on him. He made no efforts to hide it. He wanted me to
know. Sometimes he would even bring some used condoms
back with him just to get on my nerves. I was only able to
get through all that because every Monday he would leave
some money on the bedside drawer when he left. I used it
to buy food and not much else. I saved a little bit of it and
sold most of my clothes and the blankets I'd used at school.
When I had enough, I started jumping the border into
Botswana and buying *mabhero* and reselling them here. I
was doing this when one day, I came home to find Tinashe
in bed with another girl. I didn't say anything Craig. I had
no more words left.

That same week I found a house to rent and I left him soon
after. I didn't even have a bed to sleep on. Not even a reed
mat my guy. I slept on the floor. I took some cooking
utensils from Tinashe's place and his gas stove and he never
asked for them back. I guess he was just happy that he
finally got rid of me. The first thing I did was get my sister
from my uncle's house. I was afraid for her. If he had had
the nerve to do what he did on the night of Mhamha's
funeral then he could do anything even to a fourteen year
old girl. But aside from being given too much work and too
little food she said he hadn't touched her. I don't know if it's
true. She was quieter than she used to be. And she couldn't
look me in the eyes when she talked to me. But I thought if
anything had happened it was better to forget about it, so I
didn't press her anymore. Things were hard Craig. Fuck,
they still are.

All this time I'd taken a two year long break from school.
This was the same year I had to do my internship. Since I

couldn't buy and sell anymore and my sister needed school fees, I needed a paid internship. I couldn't afford to work for free. Nothing good came up until I got an interview at this bank. I knew if I got it, I would get double the pay that most accounting internships paid, the ones that paid at all. God! I needed that job you have to understand. After the interview, the boss, this potbellied, bald, ball of a man who was like well in his fifties, he tells me I'd done okay but there were other better interviewees. But, he says, he can help me out, that we can help each other out. I thought about my baby. I thought about my sister. I thought about the skeleton lying in that coffin. I thought about my uncle in the dark room that smelled like shit and vomit and death. I thought about Tinashe in bed with that girl. I thought about sleeping on the cold hard floor. I had nothing left to lose. I'd already been humiliated and degraded and used. And for what? At least this time my baby got to have a future. She got to have food on her plate. She could sleep in a comfortable bed. My sister could go back to school. I agreed to do whatever he wanted. So, I go to work. Every once in a while, he calls me into his office and closes the door. I don't say anything as he unzips his trousers and I get down on my knees. Sometimes he tells me to go to a certain lodge during lunch break. He arrives a few minutes later. Afterwards I shower but I can never get the stale smell of my uncle's sweat off of me.

[15/06, 21:23] **Anesu:** So this is my story Craig. Is it fucked up enough for you? I'm sorry but I just needed to speak out. I've been silent for so long. I don't know if you'll even read all of this. I know it's a lot. If you don't, it's okay. I feel a little better for having written it. But if you do, I hope you won't judge me. I did what I had to. And most of all, don't pity me. Or if you do, don't say you're sorry. It doesn't help me. It just makes me feel even more miserable. It'll be enough to know that you listened, like you always did.

[15/06, 21:59] CeeTheScribe: I read all of it. I honestly don't know what to say since I'm not allowed to say sorry. How is your daughter? And your sister?

[15/06, 22:01] Anesu: They're okay. Ru is about a year old now. Knowing she's at home waiting for me is the only thing that gets me through the day. My sister, I don't know. She just keeps to herself.

[15/06, 22:02] CeeTheScribe: That's good to hear. About the baby I mean.

[15/06, 22:04] CeeTheScribe: So listen, uhm, I work at this engineering firm and the manager is a close friend of my dad's. If you want, I'm sure I can get him to let you come for an interview. I know you're pretty capable so I'm sure you'll get it. I don't know how much you'll get paid though.

[15/06, 22:05] Anesu: Wait what!? Are you serious?

[15/06, 22:06] CeeTheScribe: I wouldn't joke about this

[15/06, 22:08] Anesu: OMG okay. I wasn't expecting that. Yes of course I want it! Thank you, Craig. Thank you so much. I'm literally crying right now. I can't believe this! I always knew being friends with you was a good idea kkkk.

[15/06, 22:09] CeeTheScribe: Lol don't make me regret this now. Anyways I'm going to turn in. Thanks for sharing all this with me. I wish there was more I could do to help you. Goodnight

[15/06, 22:10] **Anesu**: Goodnight. And again, thank you so so much. I don't know how I'll ever repay you for this.

[15/06, 22:10] **CeeTheScribe**: You don't need to. You deserve this

***

[09/07, 11:03] **+263 799 676 728:** Hello. It's Anesu's sister. I don't know how to even tell you this. I still can't believe it myself. Anesu was in a car accident on her way back from work yesterday. She is at Parirenyatwa Hospital right now and she hasn't woken up yet. I thought I should let you know because she talked a lot about how you helped her. Visiting hours start at 4pm. I hope your will come.

[09/07, 11:03] **+263 799 676 728:** *you

A Bed of Injustice

The empty space next to her felt too expansive. The absence of Rewai, her husband of fifty years, weighed on her heavier than it had on previous nights when he had not shared her bed with her. She longed more than ever to reach out and feel his stolid sturdiness, a quality of his that had served as a tether whenever her own emotions became so overwhelming that they threatened to draw her to some place far away.

A sombre nostalgia caressed her bones; a wistful reminiscence of the nights when he had lain next to her, nights when he had quietly rolled her over and pressed himself upon her, gently, tenderly, as if she were the most fragile thing in the world. In those moments she felt between the layers of the connection that bound them, a secret dimension, their own private sanctuary, populous with feelings that she knew his manhood would not allow him to express and words that she accepted were too sentimentally feminine for her to utter.

Her memory extracted her from the present and cast her fifty-one years back, the first time she had laid eyes on him. She was sixteen, uninitiated in the pangs that come with loving someone and sharing a life. He came to Bharabhara, the colloquial name for St. Barbara's, her growth point township, from St. James, a small village on the other side of Nyamhemba Mountain. He was part of a soccer team that was to play in an annual tournament which was being hosted by their local side, The Bharabhara Warriors, given the honour of doing so because they were the defending champions. He immediately stood out, with his skin which was the colour of a *roro* fruit and his thick head of hair that was much darker than the sun-browned hair of everyone she had ever seen. That, and the almost perfectly symmetrical oval shape of his face made her turn and scratch her friend's shoulder and say, "Look at that boy. He is beautiful. Not handsome *ba* no. Beautiful." They broke out in laughter, loud guffawing sounds that had the practiced gaiety of excited teenage virgins who wanted to draw attention to themselves without being too conspicuous.

She was surprised, after the tournament ended, when a girl came and asked to speak with her. She recalled having seen the girl around a few times although she did not know her name. The girl introduced herself as Serbia and was the beautiful boy's cousin, the daughter of his mother's sister. Serbia told her that her cousin had seen her and taken a liking to her and was interested in starting up a relationship with her. She declined his advance. She was currently going to school, wanted to focus on her books and did not want anything to do with boys but she feared, from the look of amusement on Serbia's face, that her objection had been too needlessly long winded and gave away her true inclination.

A week later, she met Serbia again at the village well. Serbia had relayed her message to her cousin and he had said that he was in love with her, and he was prepared to wait for her to finish school before marrying her. He, himself, was currently working in Salisbury as a cook for a white man, and the money that the white man gave him would be enough for him to be able to pay her lobola by the time she graduated secondary school. His patience had impressed her, the fact that he was willing to let her, a girl, finish school. She had already been charmed by his looks and to completely alleviate her uncertainty, Serbia handed her four half-crown coins.

Even though she said she would think about it – because it was customary for a girl to refuse a man's preliminary advances – the jingle of the silver coins as they landed onto her palm was the melody that soundtracked the start of their relationship.

She returned to school after the holiday and there she was the envy of many girls, in part due to the billets-doux that he sometimes sent her, but mostly because of the coins that would sometimes "accidentally" drop out of the brown envelopes that she made sure she opened only in full view of an audience. While she was at school, he informed his parents about his prospects. They had got to the point where their hints about wanting a daughter-in-law from their eldest son had evolved to outright requests, so they did not object to the fact that they had to wait for one more year to finally have their *muroora*. They, in turn, wasted no time approaching her family for the asking. By the time she finished writing her last exams, it was already time for the ceremony of counting the cattle after which she would officially become his wife.

***

When she had left him in the hut that night as she went to bed, she had been hoping that he would finally join her. It was, after all, the seventh day that her junior wife, Lucia, had not been at home. For the six previous nights he had not come to her. She had stood in the doorway for a long time, watching him as he sat on his favourite wooden stool that their son, Chari, had carved for him as part of his woodwork project in secondary school. He liked to stay behind after everyone had gone to their sleeping quarters and sit close to the fire, so close that his feet would partially cross over the threshold of the hearth and into the ash and she often had to remind him to wipe them before he climbed into bed with her. He would sit for hours in the dim orange glow of the embers, long after the fire had exhausted itself, sometimes as far into the night as midnight, arms folded in his lap and eyes closed, lost in that blurred land between sleep and being awake. She found it odd, this custom of his, and she wondered what thoughts haunted him in that quiet darkness.

She did derive a small, complacent kind of pleasure, the kind that comes from inconsequential internal victories, from the fact that he liked to do his meditations in her hut rather than her co-wife's. She was unsure whether he chose to do so because of her status as senior wife or it was simply out of habit, having been married to only her for thirty-three years before he took his second wife. Another possibility still, was simply that her hut was larger and airier, but since that particular explanation did not bring with it any sort of self-satisfaction, she brushed it aside hastily. Even on the days when he went to eat in Lucia's hut, after his meal he would leave her smaller, thatched round kitchen on the far side of the compound and come to her nearly identical but larger one on the opposite end, trudging with the deliberate lack of urgency of a man who had power over both the things behind and ahead of him.

From the stagnant silence that shrouded the night, she estimated that it was some time in the early morning hours, maybe around one or two. There was the kind of eerie calm that only comes when the world holds its breath as the things that roam the nights come out of their shadowed homes. She stretched her hand out into the darkness. It was met with the hollow coldness of a void where he should have been lying. It stung, knowing that he opted to go and sleep alone in the bed of his junior wife rather than with her. She had wanted to ask him why, when she was watching him from the door that night, but the question could not escape the cage of uxorial subservience, a cage whose walls were fortified by five decades of servitude. In spite of the circumstances leading to Lucia's departure, she had not been able to stifle the small sense of elation that she would once again have him to herself, the way it used to be, the way it was supposed to be. So she had felt slighted when on the first night of her absence, she did not hear the familiar dragging of feet which always signified his arrival. She waited. And waited. But he did not come.

Thinking about her co-wife, a familiar feeling began to creep into her gut: jealousy. It slithered up her spine, coiling itself around it, its scaly skin wet and chilly and it made her skin tighten. She knew it too well, this sensation. She had endured it for seventeen years. It had visited her on nights that she lay alone in her bed, foraging through the past and wandering to a reality where her life had taken a different trajectory. It whispered venomously into her mind, its voice icy and cutting and its breath acidic. *Is he as gentle with her as he used to be with you? Does he take her with the same desperate need that he once took you with? Or is their intimacy dispassionate, a frugal exercise in the fulfilment of conjugal obligation? Does he hold her afterwards or does he roll away and sleep with his back to her the same way he does with you, repulsed by your wrinkled skin and your sagged breasts? What secrets are there, lingering in the air of their little bedroom?*

***

Lucia's arrival into their life was like a candle suddenly going out on a dark night. It slowly took apart their marriage, breaking down the comfort and security that had been built over three decades, scattering the pieces about her until even she could not recognize what it had once been.

When she first heard the story, she was pregnant with Chari. It was her second pregnancy in the eleven years since their first daughter, Sekai, was born. By that time, chatter about her failure to bear more children and give her husband a son had risen to a deafening decibel. It was everywhere; at the river where she washed her clothes and bathed, at the monthly village meetings, at church. It was loudest, however, under the roof of her in-laws' house, tucked discreetly behind closed doors or scattered about at family gatherings. So she had been overjoyed when she discovered that she was expecting. She started to go about the village advertising her new status to everyone. At the river, a woman would ask, "How are you? How are they at home?"

And she would reply, "Everyone is well *mhaiyo*. We are all excited about the new baby that is coming."

The other woman would immediately brighten, anticipating being the recipient of the latest bit of village gossip, before she asked, "What baby? Is someone expecting?"

She would raise her hand and caress her belly before saying, "Me. I am pregnant."

"Ehuu glory to God *kani* Maa Sekai *iwe*. Congratulations!"

Then she would tell them, if they failed to ask, that she was two months along before proceeding to recount a dream she had had the day that she discovered she was pregnant. In it, she was being charged by an enormous bull and she concluded that this meant that the baby would be a boy. Because of this, when her father-in-law, Baba Tagwirei, summoned her and Rewai to his homestead, she had assumed it was to offer some sort of congratulations. Maybe slaughter a goat in their honour or at the very least, a chicken.

She was slightly puzzled when they arrived and found Rewai's entire family gathered inside the smoky hut; Baba Tagwirei and Mhai Sekesai, his parents; Rewai's younger brothers, Maziwangei and Razaro; his younger sister, Fatima and the two wives of his brothers Maa Chido and Maa Chipo, the names of whose children she sometimes got mixed up. The only person who was absent was Rewai's elder sister who was married to a man who lived in a village far away from St James and had been unable to come on such short notice. There were also three elderly men whom she did not recognize.

Her attention, however, rested on a strange looking woman who was sitting on the *chikuwa*, the earthen ancestral altar that was built against the wall at the front of the hut. The woman's head was crowned by a mop of dusty brown dreadlocks, decorated with an assortment of shells and beads and twigs. She wore a rosary around her neck that was beaded with the bones of some small creature, a horn shaped pendant the size of a finger dangling at her chest. Cloaking her large frame were layers of dirty black cloth that were tattered at the edges that grazed her grime crusted bare feet.

Her head was bowed but she kept jerking it intermittently from side to side as if she was being startled repeatedly by sounds that only she could hear and she was muttering something through her smoke blackened lips. She was cradling a baby in her arms who seemed strangely unperturbed by the odd behaviour of its custodian. Apart from her appearance, it was also unheard of, downright blasphemous, for any person, a woman and a stranger nonetheless, to sit on the sacred ancestral altar. Only the head of the household, or his sons if he was deceased, was allowed to kneel in front of it when he was communing with the spirits of the ancestors.

She took her place amongst the rest of the women on the floor and waited for her husband to initiate the greetings. A brief ruckus ensued as they all simultaneously beat their cupped hands together and asked after each other's health and the wellbeing of each other's families. After that, a thick uneasy silence settled on the small kitchen, disturbed occasionally by the strange woman's incoherent mumbling.

Everyone turned to Baba Tagwirei. For a long while, he kept his eyes fixated on some point on the floor at his feet, pondering how best to begin. Eventually he looked up and slowly reached into his breast pocket. He took out a small black wooden snuff box, the varnish on the edges corroded from frequent use. He knocked some of the powdered tobacco into his palm. With a tremulous right hand, he took a pinch and snorted through each nostril. He sneezed loudly, the force catapulting his frail body backwards and making it clutter against the wall of the hut. He rubbed the remainder of the snuff between his hands and then into his kinky grey hair. His watery, cataracted eyes, now bloodshot, scanned the room before he finally cleared his throat and began to explain the presence of their visitors.

He spoke carefully, manoeuvring the past with the measured wariness of one traversing an unfamiliar territory. "Ehhh…" he began, "…these men you see here are from the Mbinde family. I am sure you all know the name. They are the chiefs down there in Gandanzara. Ehhh across the Nyatande river. Close to Osbourne Dam. Is that not so?" The three men nodded simultaneously in confirmation, an off-key concord of bobbing heads.

"Now what they tell me happened a long time ago, when even my grandfather still suckled on the breast of his mother, before the arrival of the men without knees. Ehhh so what happened is this: one of ours went in search of a hearth to warm himself in their home. His name was Tsindimbewa. And he found himself a woman amongst their people. But because he had no kraal, he could not pay the *roora*, so he had to work for them for some time before he could take his bride home. That is how it was done in those days. Ehhh as these things go, it so happened that there was a war between these… the Mbindes and another tribe and Tsindimbewa was killed in their home before he could take his bride. Am I correct?" The heads bobbed once more.

"Now, because Tsindimbewa's blood was spilled in their home and he did not get what was due to him, his spirit has come back. Ehhh I am speaking of *ngozi*. It has wreaked havoc on them and a lot of misfortune has befallen their family in recent years. After they consulted this spirit medium, this woman who you see sitting there…" he gestured in the general direction of the strange woman sitting on the altar, careful not to point at her, "…she has told them that to resolve this matter, Tsindimbewa's wife must be brought here to his home and only then will their debt be repaid. Is that so?"

"And the son." It was one of the three men, the eldest looking of them, whose eyes were sunken deep into their sockets and whose head was bald.

"Ah yes yes. Forgive me, these teeth have chewed many Christmases, my memory is not as sharp as it used to be. Ehhh the woman that they bring to us must bear a son and he must be given the name Tsindimbewa. After that she is free to stay here or go back to her people if she wishes. Ehhh I think this time I have said everything, is it not so?" When everyone murmured their agreement, he then went on to explain the arrangement they had made, the one that would undo her and Rewai's twenty-one years of matrimony. Each syllable felt like Baba Tagwirei was pulling a thread from the fabric of her life, unravelling it.

"Ehhh that baby that you see there in the hands of the medium is the compensation that they have brought us. There will be a ceremony also where they will brew beer and put a bull into our kraal. But all of this can come later. For now, they have brought us Tsindimbewa's bride. Ehhh as the eldest member of the family she was to come to me, but you can see that she is still on her mother's breast. By the time she comes of age I will no longer be strong enough. So I have decided that she will go to Rewai, my eldest son. The girl can stay in my home for now. I will take care of her until the time comes that she is able to fulfil her duties."

She tried her best to care for Lucia or at the very least to be impartial, to understand that nothing was her fault and that she was as much of a victim of the same circumstances as herself. She fed her when she came to play with her own children. She bathed her. She did her best to be motherly. But something had wound itself around her neck, that day Lucia came, that tightened each season that passed and the girl grew, that she came closer to being a woman.

When, at fourteen, Lucia came and told her that she had bled, she wept that night. She mourned what she knew would effectively be the death of her marriage. When Rewai attempted to console her, his efforts only served to fuel her grief with anger. It was unfair. Why did she have to bear the consequences of the actions of some men who had lived and died in some faraway land and a faraway time? She had done and been everything a good wife was supposed to do and be and yet, that had not been enough to keep her home.

That year the Mbindes came once again. They were shown a plot of land to build a hut and a house for Rewai's soon to be bride. After it was completed, there was a drinking ceremony and she and all the daughters and daughters in law took Lucia into her new hut where they explained to her that she was now a woman and taught her the duties she would have to perform.

Initially, Rewai was polite enough to feign impartiality, distributing his conjugal visits equally between her and Lucia. He ate both the plates of sadza that they set before him, even favouring hers because she was the more experienced cook. But as time went by, her edge over Lucia slowly began to slip away. As Lucia got older, she became better at making her own household more attractive to their shared husband, making it almost as good as hers. Where her age had once been advantageous it started to become a handicap. She was becoming old while her junior wife was transforming from a girl into an attractive young woman. She could not compete with her youthful beauty and vigour. She was now a relic, an ancient artefact that her husband only appreciated out of nostalgic sentiment while Lucia was his new exciting jewel. She looked on helplessly as the nights that he spent with her became fewer each passing month and he no longer made love to her. Eventually, she was grateful to have him come at all, once a week or sometimes once a fortnight, only as a courtesy.

When Lucia became pregnant, she dared to hope that her child was a boy so that Lucia could go back to her people. She prayed to God, to the ancestors, to anyone who would listen. She helped her to look for herbs that would ensure the child would be a boy. Her naïve junior wife took this to be well wishing. She was completely oblivious to the resentment that was harboured towards her. But Lucia had a daughter. Lucia had four daughters over the following nine years. And with each birth she grew more resentful of both Lucia and her children.

A bitterness planted itself inside her, nurtured by each night that she waited for Rewai to come to her, by each of Lucia's births, each event bringing with it yet another disappointment. It rooted itself in her mind and its gnarly branches spread throughout her body. Her heart festered under the shadow it cast over her, turning into an ugly putrid lump. It was this bitterness, her attempt to free herself of it that had driven her to go to the medicine man.

She turned again in her bed. It was the fourth time she had woken up and now her bedroom was faintly illuminated by the murky luminescent tinge of dawn. She climbed out of the bed and slid open the bottom drawer of her bedside cabinet. Her bones groaned and creaked as she bent down and reached inside. She rummaged through her slips and underwear until her fingers grazed the soft, leathery skin of the cow hide pouch that the medicine man had given her. She held it by the string that was wound around its neck and extended her arm to hold it as far away from her as she could before she got up and walked to the outhouse as briskly as her arthritic legs would allow. With trembling fingers, she untied the little bag, being careful not to spill any of its contents on herself. She knew one needed to ingest the mystical white powder for its magic to affect them, but after she had witnessed what it did to Lucia the very idea of even touching it now terrified her.

It had been easy enough to get Lucia to take it. She knew her junior wife was particularly fond of eggs so she cooked several of them and then put one aside, which she seasoned with the powder.

"This is good *muti*," the small, shifty looking man had assured her. "It will make your problem go away..." he snapped his fingers, "...like that."

She had waited for Lucia to pass by on her way to fetch water at the well. She invited her in and offered her the tainted egg.

"This is very good *maikuru*. What did you put in it?" Lucia licked her fingers as she gave the compliment.

"I did not use anything at all. *Inga* you know when it comes to pots no one can stand with me. I was born with the *shawi* of cooking." She searched Lucia's face for any kind of distortion, any sign that would hint that she had not been conned but she saw only the younger woman's savour. When three days passed and there was still no change in Lucia's behaviour, she knew that the medicine man had tricked her.

On the fourth day, she woke up to Rewai banging loudly on her bedroom door which she had resigned herself to locking, an effort to deceive her mind into thinking that keeping him away was her choice.

"Come. Hurry up. Something has happened to Lucia."

When she got out Lucia was standing in the middle of the yard, naked as the day she was born. Her head was thrown back and she was staring at the sky as if she were in a trance. She was shivering.

"I tried putting some clothes on her but she kept kicking me away. Help me with her."

They started to walk towards Lucia. Abruptly, she turned to face them. The serenity that had been masking her face began to contort into an angry scowl. Her arm shot up. A shaky finger pointed at them. However, she could not help feeling as if Lucia's noxious glare was focused on her. "Look!" Lucia shrieked.

Her heart leapt.

"See me. I said see me! I have come. You will pay. I said you will all pay. They plucked the egg from the lion's roost. They ran away with it across the starless sky. They threw it into the lake. Amongst the weeds and the crocodiles. *Yowee kani!* The river runs red with blood and bones. Oh you who dwell in the sky, see me! You see what happens under these roofs; what happens in the dark. I am your child. I am your bride. Turn these stones over. There are maggots crawling underneath. Above them. Everywhere. They are everywhere, do you hear? The pigs will eat them all up. I have finished. *Maiwee kani* I am finished." As suddenly as she had started, she stopped and went limp once more. Rewai took an uncertain step towards her. Without warning, she turned and fled. He hesitated briefly before he followed after her.

She remained glued in place, stunned. She had not expected this. She had not truly believed that anything would happen. More than anything, she had gone to see the medicine man to indulge her jealousy. It was why she had not asked for further details when the man did not tell her what exactly would happen aside from the vague promise that her problem would go away.

She looked around quickly before she allowed a smile to creep onto her face.

When Rewai finally brought Lucia back, it was she who had suggested that they take her to *mapositori*, the men from the apostolic church who wore white garments and were known for their healing abilities because they could deal with both the things of faith and the things of spirits. "They know how best to deal with these things Baa Sekai," she crooned. He took Lucia the next day, a rope tethered to her waist in case she tried to run away again. He stayed with her there that night and only returned the next afternoon. At first, she thought the change she saw in his demeanour was simply fatigue – there was a visible weariness about him. But over the following days she began to sense that it was more, something that had made him recoil from her and treat her with a coolness that he had not shown her even after Lucia's arrival.

She emptied the contents of the pouch into the latrine before she let the bag drop in. When she walked out something compelled her to look towards Lucia's hut. Rewai was standing in the doorway, hands thrust deep into his pockets, watching her.

A Family Meeting

The living room, no matter how many times I had been there in the past, always felt unwelcoming. I am not sure why. Perhaps it was the way that it was excessively spacious, almost palatial, with its tall walls and high ceiling that made it feel hollow and empty. It gave me this feeling that everything inside, especially the people, were far away. The minimalistic approach that Mary had taken with the décor only compounded that feeling. Or maybe it was because of the full-length windows which span the entire north facing wall that let in too much light. I could not help feeling as if I was exposed, under observation and even my most private things, my thoughts, were on display. Maybe I simply did not like being there. It was apparent that, of all my siblings, my brother, Mukoma John, and his wife were fond of me the least. That, after all, was why they chose to take my younger sister instead of me to live with them in the city after their daughter was born, even though I certainly would have been the better nanny.

The lavishness of the house also added to my discomfort. I felt like an alien object in there. Located in Shawasha Hills, one of the most exclusionary suburbs in Harare, my brother's house is a monument to the excessive indulgence of those who sit at the upper echelons of society, just like others like it that are almost a staple when you venture towards the fringes of Harare East. That part of the city is where politicians and "businessmen" with government connections live. Men like Mukoma John. I once heard from a woman whose husband works as a security guard in the area, that one of Mugabe's children lived there. Towering over almost a hectare of evergreen manicured lawn with a tennis-cum-basketball court and a heated swimming pool, with its seven bedrooms and two stories, it is a far cry from the small, stuffy two rooms that I rent with my husband in Mabvuku that always smells like the last meal we had. Usually *sadza* and *covo* or some eggs or *matemba* on a good day.

It is evident that a great deal of attention has been given to the furnishing choices, yet in spite of this, or maybe because of it, the place seems to lack a certain cordiality that makes a home a *home*. There are none of the usual decorations one would expect to see in a typical Zimbabwean house, no family or wedding photos, no flowers or any items to pay homage to the family totem, *Nyati*, the buffalo. Several paintings hang on the white walls, abstract splashes of colour on mostly white canvasses that I find tasteless. The sofas, black and made of genuine leather – Mary makes certain everyone knows this – inexplicably lack any cushions. The light grey porcelain tiles on the floor are uncarpeted. The living room is divided into two, with a reading area on one side with a black coffee table in the middle surrounded by four footstools on either side which are their own shade of grey, two settees set against the wall to the left, an ottoman – grey as well, a bookshelf that, true to my brother's tastes, contains mostly books about wealth, power and post-colonial Africa. Runako, my daughter, was concentrating on her colouring book on the table, her tongue sticking out slightly as she wielded a water colour in her small palm like she was holding a knife. I noted to myself that I needed to take her to Mai Trevor's to get her hair redone.

I, myself, was sitting on the other side of the room, in the middle of the lounging area, like a human centrepiece, and my family was on the sofas surrounding me. If I'd been feeling kinder to myself, I would have interpreted the bitter looks in their eyes as judgement. Judgement is situational, fleeting, an unspoken reproach for having done something wrong – but not unacceptable. But I was not feeling kind to myself. Not in that place. Not with those people. And what I saw in their eyes, at least in Mukoma John's and Mary's, in my elder sister's, Sisi Pedzi, reflected the same emotion that was searing within me; that was making waves in my body like a shiver: contempt.

They claimed they only wanted to help me.

It was my mother who had convinced me to go to the meeting. But that did not explain why she was the only one not sitting on the sofas with everyone else. Mhaiyo had taken a stool and was sitting just behind me, to my left. I could not see her from my position on the floor, except for the fringe of her wrapper, the maroon one that she always takes with her when she comes to Harare; the one with the golden trim at the hem. I could feel the warmth of her skin, smell the scent of earth and smoke that always clung to her clothes no matter how many times they were washed. If it were not for her I would not have been there listening to their nonsense. I wanted to just get up and walk away. In fact, I was already starting to get up when I felt a gentle touch on my shoulder.

I looked up at Mhaiyo's sad face. The wrinkles of her withered skin seemed to have deepened, a forlorn warmth flowing in its folds that calmed me down. Her mouth was curled slightly at the corners in a weak attempt at a smile that did not reach her eyes. I took a deep breath and turned towards the other people in the room.

They were led by Mukoma John. He was seated at the helm of what I then realised was some kind of sequential arrangement, in descending order of their perceived importance. It was no coincidence that they had chosen to sit themselves that way. Mukoma John often liked to remind everyone that he was the head of the family, a title I would gladly let him have if he did not spend every family gathering lamenting how dependent everyone was on him. One day, during one of his outbursts, he compared himself to Carpenter, our father's ox that I famously heard had single handedly saved the family during the drought of '92. It had conjured an image of him, yoke on his shoulders, wearing nothing but his underwear, his paunch hanging in front of him, as he pulled a scotch cart in which our entire family sat. Naturally, I laughed. I was maybe eleven or twelve at the time. He had heard me and, looking pained and grave, he quoted the Bible, "They will mock Him and spit on Him, and scourge Him and kill Him," which had made me laugh even more. I didn't think it was possible for someone to change colour like a chameleon until I saw how dark his face got that day.

Mukoma John did not earn the title because of any kind of seniority, being the third of our parents' children after our eldest brother, Chakanetsa, whom I never got to meet, and Sisi Pedzi who, I noted with indifference, sat in third place. Nor was it particularly his concern for the well-being of our family. Aside from having sent my younger sister and I to school and occasionally having to chip in the larger share of money for family events, he mostly took no interest in our lives. However, he was our father's only living son. He was also, as an extension of the privilege that came with that status, the most successful in our family, the only one that had gone to university and he held a Master's degree in some field that I don't allow myself to care enough to remember. Sisi Pedzi only went as far as O level before she had to get a job so that she could support Mukoma John's education. As such, he was the most financially equipped to resolve the issues and scandals that seemed to ceaselessly plague our family, and he took charge after our father died almost six years ago.

Next to Mukoma John, occupying two thirds of the two-seater sofa, is his wife, our family's jewel, Mary. Traditionally, she should have ranked only higher than her daughters in the hierarchy, but we took exception to her. You see, she is no ordinary *muroora*. She was white, an American. Other people bragged about their family members going overseas. Well, Mukoma John brought overseas to us. It irked me to see how everyone bent over for her as if being a white wife accorded her some special authority; authority that remained unchallenged even by her husband, whom I suspect, could not fathom doing anything to potentially upset his most valuable trophy from his overseas travels. He imported her after he finished his Master's degree. They were engaged six months after they met and married a month afterwards. Mary is obese, a word that is as foreign to me as the country from which she came – I could never think of a Zimbabwean as being obese – with thin blonde hair that looks like the wisps on a premature maize cob, through which an egg-white scalp can be seen through the line where her hair is parted. Her sun-freckled skin is a ripe red that looks so tender, I think that if I poked it, it wouldn't be too dissimilar to poking a tomato that has been left in the sun for too long.

After Mary, there was Sisi Pedzi, the *tete* of the family, the eldest paternal aunt. The role suited her perfectly. She liked to be a part of everything and ordered people around. She worked at the CVR and she had the irritability and impatience to match. Then there was Munashe, Mukoma John's son with whom I got along quite well and whose discomfort I could sense from the distant expression on his face and the way he avoided meeting my eyes as if I were a solar eclipse. I knew that if he had had any say, he would not have been there, but his father had likely insisted that he attend. He kept fidgeting in his seat, frequently shuffling his crossed legs. The rest of the succession was completed by my younger sister and then my niece, both sitting quietly, holding their faces in their laps, only occasionally glancing at each other nervously whenever Sisi Pedzi interjected with a, "you two girls should not make the same mistake, do you hear?" which she had done three times already.

The so called 'mistake' was my decision to leave my husband.

It was not the first time that I had wanted to do so. I was married to Addmore for four years. That dog tries to stick his thing in anything that wears a skirt like an animal during the mating season. I could stand it when all he did was sleep around and drink too much, when the height of his delinquency could easily be washed off; could become a distant memory in the arms of another man. I could look past his being attracted to other women. I, after all, am not immune to those same impulses. I could even forgive him for perhaps having got tired of our marriage and lost interest. That feeling quickly became mutual after I learned about his affairs. Besides, if he hadn't got me pregnant, I would never have married him at all. But I couldn't just leave him before. There was Runako to consider. So I stayed. It had to be enough for me that he fed our daughter, gave her a roof to sleep under and clothes to wear. That was all I needed from him and he had mostly done it without fail. He loved Runako. He could sleep with whomever he chose and drink unto kingdom come for all I cared, as long as he was a father to our child. But then, without warning or explanation, a few months ago, he just stopped. No more grocery. No more gifts and snacks for Runako when he came home. He started acting as if she had suddenly ceased to exist. And when I confronted him about it, he nearly killed me.

I looked once again at the play area, the effort to open my swollen left eye making my headache. Runako was not there anymore. Momentarily panicking, I twisted my body suddenly to look behind me and a sharp jab of pain pierced the right side of my ribcage and made my vision momentarily dark. I bit my lower lip to stop myself from screaming and the metallic taste of blood filled my mouth. I had forgotten about the tear on my lip. Tenderly, I ran my tongue over the wound and then sucked on it until it stopped bleeding. Clenching my jaws and digging my nails into my thighs, I swallowed. More carefully, I turned around to look for my daughter. Runako was standing in the archway that led into the living room from the foyer.

I had not told anyone, except Mhaiyo, the reason I wanted to leave Addmore. She was the only other person who openly expressed her disapproval of the way Mukoma John insisted on asserting himself over everything and everyone. So it had come as a surprise to me, after I told her what had happened, when she had said that we needed to talk about the issue with Mukoma John and that it was imperative that we go to his house the very next day. As I listened, Mhaiyo had told my brother over the phone that I was going to leave my husband and then added, peculiarly, that she would tell him more in person. After she hung up, I asked her why she had done that.

Instead of answering my question, she asked, rather oddly because it had been some time since I had arrived, "And where do you think you have left my granddaughter?"

For a moment, a panicking feeling, seized me, a murky, dark sensation that something was suddenly very wrong; the same one I had been getting whenever Runako was mentioned and I could not immediately find her. It started about the same time Addmore began his negligent behaviour. And then I remembered that I had left her with my husband. Mhaiyo gave me a strange look before she repeated that he needed to go and see Mukoma John urgently.

So at sunrise, we boarded a lorry from Murehwa to Harare and during the entire drive, my mother held my hand, an unusually physical display of affection from a woman who, as far as I could recall, had only ever hugged me the day that our father died. When we arrived at Mukoma John's house, I was surprised to see Runako there.

After I arrived, everyone kept looking at me as if I had sat on something that smelled and did not know it, and more than once I felt the urge to leave, to just sneak out, but

Mhaiyo did not leave me alone for a moment. Breakfast was eaten in silence, a small serving of bacon, garlic bread, scrambled eggs and orange juice that Mhaiyo, who insisted that a meal could not be called breakfast if there was no white tea, barely touched. Soon after, I was called into the living room by my niece, whom I noticed, was unusually quiet and tense. I found a blanket folded on the floor in the centre of the room and Mhaiyo sitting on a chair next to it.

"You cannot leave your husband, Prudence." It was Mukoma John. He does not beat around the bush. For all his shortcomings, it is one quality of his that I like.

"And why is that Mukoma John. Please tell me why, according to you, I cannot leave my own husband." My head was already starting to feel like a boiling pot.

"Because he paid his *roora*."

"So what? Am I a store item that cannot be returned? If this is why you have brought me here, to gang up on me about this, I will not hear it. I will get up and go right now."

"Prudence, for Runako's sake listen to us. We only want to help you." The mention of my daughter's name calmed me down. A brief silence had followed and it was then that I noticed how uncomfortable the room made me feel.

My brother's voice droned on, his words weaving into each other monotonously, one indistinguishable from the next so that all I heard was a continuous hum, aware only of the movement of his lips. Looking at him more closely I began to notice, for the first time, the bags under his eyes, the stubble of hair on his face that was already showing some white, the way his hair was starting to thin at the temples. As I watched his dry lips rise and fall and contort, I imagined the words he must be saying. Some iteration of the same thing he always says over and over again. *I am the head of this family and it is my duty to look after you. I only want to help you. I know what is best for you and everyone else because I have been abroad and I have a stick between my legs.* Suddenly I felt tired. I yawned loudly, without bothering to cover my mouth.

"Prudence." I looked up. Mary's eyes were the colour of honey. "Please listen to your brother. We all just want what's best for you. We all get that this situation isn't ideal and personally, I can't imagine what you're going through right now, but we're all here for you. We just want to help you."

I wondered what kind of help this white woman could offer me. This woman who was, just by being what she was, a treasure, a prize, in the eyes of not only her husband, but the rest of the family as well. This woman that was treated like an egg as if she would break at the slightest provocation. How could she help me? Had she not just admitted that she could not possibly fathom what I was going through. So what could she do for me if she did not even understand my situation?

"*Mainini,* you can talk and talk until your mouth becomes dry and I will listen, but we will end up in the same place that we started. You are wasting your time and mine. I have made my decision. You do not know what I have gone through at the hands of that man. You were not there when he beat me the way you would beat a donkey that was refusing to walk, until I fainted. I did not want to come here about this matter because I knew that you would not understand. You never understand. You live here in this big house on this hill and you have no clue what life is like for the rest of us who live down there. I have only come here as a courtesy to Mhaiyo. If you people want to help me, you should respect my decision or if you cannot do that then leave me alone, please *ndapota*."

Mary opened and closed her mouth several times like a fish that had been taken out of water before she turned towards Mukoma John for support.

I watched him, following his movements like a predator stalking its prey. He leaned forward on the sofa and placed a hand on his wife's which were clasped together in her lap before quickly withdrawing it. He scratched his head, the way our father used to do when he was thinking of what to say. He rubbed his chin and then cleared his throat. "What your *mainini* is saying is that if we are going to help you we need to know exactly what happened. Tell us why you have decided what you have decided and then we can see if there is something we can do to show you where you might be getting a little lost. If we know what happened at the beginning, then maybe we can show you how to resolve all of this. Is that not so Mary?" Mary's head bobbed up and down.

I was suddenly aware that I was laughing. A hooting sound like a hyena with my head thrown back, ignoring the discomfort that the movement caused me. It was now they wanted to know of the beginning? "*Wuuri*! Laugh out loud Prudence, daughter of the *Nyati*. Laugh now because these people will kill you with their words. The beginning? *Heede*."

Was my brother not the one that had boycotted the day that my husband had gone to *Babamudiki* to pay my *roora*. My own brother! Had he not said he would not have anything to do with me and my husband even after the scandal about who had got me pregnant was resolved. The word he had actually used was prostitute. He said I was "like a bitch that was fucked by every dog in the village." And *now* he wanted to ask me about the beginning?

After all, had they all not assumed they knew my story anyway. Without any inquiry, any benefit of doubt, they had always assumed that I was the one responsible for all my problems with my husband. Even though I tried to explain that my husband, too, was unfaithful, I was dismissed as always. Somehow, it was ok for him to do so because, once again, "he had paid his *roora*." So what? Mukoma John had not paid *roora* for his foreign wife so did that mean he could not order her around and treat her however he wanted? When I asked him the question all his blood went to his eyes, the way it did when he was angry, and he mumbled that it was not the same thing.

"Pee, you are not the first woman that has been beaten by her husband and you will not be the last. Yet all the other women stay because they understand what it takes to keep a home together; what a woman needs to endure for her family's sake. It is not easy being a woman. It never has been and it never will be. You just need to understand that and the sooner you do, the easier everything becomes. The only way you can be happy is by keeping your husband happy. But you *manje*, you think that there is something special about you. You think you are clever, but the truth is you are very foolish. And knowing you the way I do, it is probably you who aggravated him. I know you Pee. You are rowdy and you do not show respect and submissiveness to the people who have authority over you. I have seen the way you talk to your husband, as if he is your equal, the way you used to talk to Baba and the way you are now talking to Mukoma John here. Always so disrespectful. I know your husband and he does not seem like the kind of man who would do the things you say without being provoked." Sisi Pedzi was panting by the time she finished speaking. She had inherited our father's temper but not his physique.

I could not think of an occasion where my sister had ever spoken to my husband beyond a greeting.

"But *Sisi*…"

"Shut up! I am not finished talking." The vein at the side of her head looked like it had come alive, pulsating visibly even from where I was and there was a speck of rheum at the corner of the left one which often happened when she had gone a long time without her glasses. "Do you know what Baba's last words were? Do you know?"

"I think…" She cut me off.

"He said, 'I am no longer a man in my own house.' It is because of this kind of behaviour. This disrespect. And now you want to do the same thing to me and to your brother?"

Our father's last words were in fact, "Go and fetch me some water." I was the one that took him to the hospital the morning he died. We were at the hospital gate when he suddenly complained that he was feeling lightheaded and he wanted some water. I sat him down and looked for a nearby vendor. By the time I returned, he was gone. If indeed he had said any such thing, he had not said it to me. Then maybe it was not me that he had been talking about.

"Do you know that my husband used to beat me too? Yes, it's true. Yes, that Baba Neri that you see who I have been with for thirty years. Our house was always the noisiest on the street. Even at midnight you would hear plates being thrown around and we would be shouting at each other. You see, I had a mouth on me and I did not like being told what to do. There was always this and that that I complained about. So we would fight a lot. Sometimes I would even win too, when he was drunk. But when he beat me, I did what you are doing and ran home crying. Until one day, after I got pregnant with Neri, Baba got tired of it. We were sitting in that old kitchen that we now use as a grain storage house. He sat me down and said, 'My daughter, this is no longer your home. Your husband paid me your *roora* in full and he does not owe me anything. He has no debt with me. I have eaten the cows he gave me; I have spent his money. He has not said he no longer wants you as his wife. So if he comes here and finds you what will I say? If he decides to take me to a *dare*, I will be found guilty. You do not belong here anymore. Go back and apologise to him and do what he tells you. If you want to cry, you will cry with him and he will comfort you because that is what a husband and wife do.' I did not like his words at the time and I was very angry because it felt like he was throwing me out of his house. I thought my own father had abandoned me. I had nowhere else to go, so I went back to my husband and I thought, why don't I try what Baba said? And before long we were no longer having the problems that we were having before. To this day, he has not raised a single finger to me."

I decided I'd had enough. "Oh my sister, I feel very sorry for you. That is all I can say. I have wasted my time coming to you people. I am leaving now. Mhamha, I am sorry. I know you were trying to help me but this is not going to work. Now give me my daughter so I can leave."

Runako was sitting on my lap. I did not see her come there. She looked up at me and her lips puckered the way they did when she was about to cry. She could always tell when I was upset. Suddenly, nothing else mattered. I just wanted to take her far away from there.

"No baby, don't cry. Everything is going to be ok."

Mhaiyo nudged my shoulder and I looked up at her. I was surprised to see a stream of tears on her face. I felt something lose air inside me. She was not looking at me and I thought to myself, "She cannot even look at you anymore." Her eyes were fixed on my lap.

"Prudence. My daughter." She shook her head slowly. There was something about the way she said my name that made me suddenly feel cold, like someone had removed the blankets on a cold June morning. I had a sense that I had heard the thing she was about to say before, even though I did not know what it was. All I knew was I did not want to hear it again. I opened my mouth to tell her to stop but the words did not come out. Instead, I found myself gasping for air as she said, "There is no one there my daughter. Look." She gestured her head at my lap.

I did not want to look. I tried to keep my eyes focused on Mhaiyo, to refuse to make sense of what she was saying, but I was not able to. Something took me and forced me to look down at the empty place on my lap, where Runako had been only a few seconds before. And the darkness that had shown me glimpses of itself at the mention of Runako's name before washed over me.

I remembered how empty I felt when I stared at my daughter's motionless body, as if everything inside me had been taken out. The world was swirling around me. Someone was screaming. My head did not feel like it was attached to my body. A voice that sounded very much like my own said, "You did this." It could not be real. She was just sleeping, I told myself. She was going to wake up and ask for her colouring book and I was going to give it to her. I looked around me. There was Mukoma John and Addmore. They were looking at me. I tried to search their eyes for the answer to the question I could not dare ask out loud. I wanted to know who had killed my baby.

As if to answer my question, Mukoma John lifted his hand and examined a small packet. I knew what it was. Even through my eyes which were full of tears, I could see the image of the rat lying on its back with red X's on its eyes. We had a rat problem in our house. He slid the packet into his pocket and then walked through the door. Addmore took a sheet and covered the body. There was not enough air in the room. It smelled like vomit and eggs. The eggs that we had with our *munya* for breakfast. The same eggs that I threw up. I remembered vomiting and feeling very hot. I looked around. There was a duvet that was balled up and tucked into a corner of the room. The room that wouldn't stop moving. With the screaming that wouldn't stop. I staggered forward and something held me back. I looked. The movement of my head caused everything to spin before it finally came to a gradual halt on the face of my husband. And then I remembered. The fight.

It was like any other fight we had. I was complaining about his infidelity. I had found out that he had a child with someone else. I wanted to take my daughter away. I remembered banging on a door. Yes. He had locked me in the bedroom. The pills. I only wanted to scare him. I only took a few. I didn't use all of them. I was sure of it. But the packet in Mukoma John's hand was empty. Suddenly, the screaming stopped. And then I saw the floor rise towards me.

When I opened my eyes again I was no longer in the bedroom and my clothes were wet. I was sitting on the floor. My head was painful like someone was beating me like I was a drum. I was looking at Mukoma John and Addmore. They were talking in low voices and Mukoma John kept looking at me a lot of times. He was holding something in his hand and Addmore was looking at it. I knew the look. He sometimes had it when we were walking together and a woman with a big chest passed us. His mouth was slightly open. Mukoma John opened the thing in his hand – his wallet – pulled out some US dollar notes. I tried to count them but it made me feel again like throwing up. He handed the money to Addmore. My husband clapped and took it then put it in his trousers' pocket. They shook hands and Mukoma John walked outside. When he opened the door, the light from outside momentarily blinded me. When Addmore closed the door, Runako was standing next to him. I was so relieved.

***

In the living room, Mukoma John was now speaking. He was talking to Mhaiyo. "Mhai, this matter is too delicate. If this gets out, it will not be good for me. It will not be good for this family. There are people that can use this against us. It is not a small thing that I did. I can get arrested or even worse because there are people that I have connections with that will do anything to bury this. It is no longer just about Prudence. I am also involved now."

"I hear you John, but what if he doesn't want her anymore. He never used to beat her. Maybe if we just allow her to leave him…"

"You know why he beat her. She was asking him about…" Mukoma John looked at me. He looked like he was sick. "Even so, Mhai. If that is the case it has to be him who says he doesn't want her anymore. What if we take her and he becomes angry? Who knows what he will do? He has already cost me too much."

"But can't you try and talk to him?"

Mukoma John shook his head and then held it in his hands. "I will try something. But if it does not work I might have to think of other solutions. They will not be good and my people will not be happy because it will draw too much attention. I do not want things to go that way. I also do not know who he has told about this. This will not end well. If only Prudence would just listen."

Mhaiyo turned to me, "Prudence, will you…"

I stood up. I had to bite my lip to stop myself from making a noise. I took my baby's hand and walked out of there.

A Note on the Text

Four of the stories in this collection have previously been published as follows:

A part of 'The Woman in the Red Dress' by AFREADA (February, 2021)

'A Hole in the Air' in Issue 31 of The Shallow Tales Review (January 31, 2021)

'Yesterday's Colours' by The Kalahari Review (March 30, 2021)

'A Bed of Injustice' under the title, 'A Bed of Injustice' by Munyori Literary Journal (February 2, 2021)

Despite my best attempts, a notably less humorous and admittedly less polished version of 'Jagged Pieces', my first attempt at braving the treacherous, heavy sigh inducing world of online publishing, has been rejected multiple times.

Acknowledgements

My gratitude to Samantha Vazhure, my publisher and editor for giving me this opportunity to share my work with the world.

Special thanks to these guys and gals: Darlington 'Mang' Mangwarire and Tadiwa Sinoia, the unpaid beta readers and reviewers of all my works, usually the initial drafts that I will be too tired and depressed to properly edit; to Zanele Mfiri, my biggest fan, for always asking for new stories and whom I still owe a story that has a happy ending; Ashtley (with a 'T') Gondo who always reminds me that "we move"; to Leanne Munyoro and Angelina 'Angie' Matipano who will probably be surprised that they are mentioned at all, but who gave me the confidence to start this journey; to Tichaona 'Tich' (Sorry man, I keep forgetting your surname) and Sylvester Mumba, the only two people I know with lives more depressing than mine, for showing me that it can always be worse; to my dad who is so maddening that I can do nothing except go to my room and write, who constantly tries to make me a better version of what he thinks a man should be with no success; to Dr. Fungi who almost derailed my career in its infancy by taking away the angst that has allowed these stories to be written; and to Jaime Maseko who's laughter silences the screams, for driving me to be better and believing in me. All of you are now required to buy a copy of the book.

I also want to thank the editors at Munyori Literary Journal, The Kalahari Review, AFREADA and The Shallow Tales Review who published my first stories and made me, as Sinoia once said, "Mr bigshot published author."

Lastly I would like to thank God. Thank God this is done and I can start working on something else now. Whew!

About the Author

Lazarus Panashe is a Zimbabwean writer and editor. He holds a bachelor's degree in Civil Engineering that he has not used for two years. His short fiction has been published online and in print in the anthology, 'Brilliance of Hope.' He writes from betwixt the four walls of his solitary bedroom, which unbeknownst to his family, is a portal to many worlds.

www.ingramcontent.com/pod-product-compliance
Lightning Source LLC
Chambersburg PA
CBHW020819190726
48285CB00006B/2342